TELLING TALES

TELLING TALES

FOR RISING STARS

C.N.NAGESWARA RAO

PARTRIDGE
A Penguin Random House Company

To order additional copies of this book, contact
Partridge India
000 800 10062 62
orders.india@partridgepublishing.com

www.partridgepublishing.com/india

DEDICATED TO

My parents C. S. Naidu and C. Chinatalli, my mother's
elder sister Chadaram Veeramma, who put me out
of my family profession and set me on a long course
in studies and her younger sister Yellapu Satyavathi,
who lent a helping hand in my academic odyssey.

AND

Hindustan Aeronautics Limited, the esteemed
organization in which I had the privilege to
work for long years. My present work is a
humble tribute to the great organization that
has completed seventy five glorious years and is
presently celebrating its Platinum Jubilee.

CONTENTS

ACKNOWLEDGEMENT

I wish to state that many of my friends, well wishers, peers and mentors have provided invaluable help in bringing out this book. I thank one and all of them.

I sincerely thank Sri Tenneti Sudhakar Rao, former Executive Director (HR), Hindustan Aeronautics Limited, who wrote a well crafted Foreword for my book. I thank Dr. Chadaram Bala Krishna, Sri Yellapu Ramana, Sri Pingali Sundara Rama Rao, Sri Samineni Srinivasa Rao, Smt. Samineni Sandhya and Smt. Buddha Vani Jahnavi, who read my tales and gave their valued opinions and suggestions for improvement.

I express my sincere thanks to Sri Chitukula Narasimha Reddy and his family members, who stood by me in various fields of my endeavor and Sri Marepally Sammi Reddy, who played the role of a king maker in making me President of Officers Association in HAL.

I remember with reverence association with Wg. Cdr. R. K. Chawla, Sri M. Sita Raman, Sri V. Srinivasan, Sri Chinta Rajeswara Rao, Sri B. Radhakishan, Sri M. Linga Murthy, Sri Dasaratha Atma, Sri M. Padmakar Rao, Sri R. G. Bansod, Sri K. S. N. Reddy, Sri D. V. Latkar and other senior executives, who made deep impact on me with their erudite knowledge. I thank Sri K. C. Sasidhara, Sri N.

Sameer, Sri V. Madhusudana Reddy and other associates of former HAOA, who gave me excellent support during my association activities in HAL.

I thank my former colleagues Sri S. V. Sastry, B. N. Sudarshan, Sri A. Dharma Rao, Sri A. Gangadhara Rao, Sri K. V. Reddy, Sri M. Srinivasulu, Sri G. Venkatesham, Sri M. Jitendernath Thakur, Sri K. Nagi Reddy, Sri V. C. Rami Reddy, Sri Viyyanna, Sri Vadrevu Ramaseshagiri Rao, Sri S. J. Raju, Sri P. Narasing Rao and other associates, association with whom immensely enriched my knowledge.

I take this opportunity to thank Dr. Buddha Veera Raghava Rao, Sri Buddha Srinivasa Rao, Sri Samineni Papa Rao, Sri Hanumanthu Srinivasa Rao, Sri Buddha Prakash, Sri Dadi Appa Rao, Sri Saragadam Satyanarayana, Sri Vegi Surya Prakasa Rao, Dr Malla Appa Rao, Sri Polamarasetty Ramakrishna, Sri Yellapu Sivaji, Sri Yellapu Bujji, Sri B.Tata Rao, Sri Kothari Ranga Rao and Sri Kothari Satyanarayana who were of phenomenal help to me in many of my activities.

I thank Sri Jampana Prathap and Sri Pandu Yadav, leaders of our locality and Sri J. Chennakesavulu, Sri B. Malliah, Sri K. Chandra Sekhar Reddy and other residents of our colony, who have remained a source of great help in all my activities.

I commemorate my bygone friends Karra Venkata Subba Rao, K. Satyanarayana Reddy and Tangi Sriramulu, who left behind in me unforgettable reminiscences. I pay my respects to my father-in-law Buddha Ramachandra

Rao, mother-in-law Buddha Ramanamma, well wishers B. R. Satyanarayana and Karri Ramachandra Rao.

I thank readers, who provided encouraging feedback on books published by me earlier. I find no words to express how deeply I am impressed with dedicated support that I have received from staff of M/s Partridge Publishing.

I fail in my duty, if I don't express my heartfelt thanks to my life partner Smt. C. L. Rajakumari, without the support of whom, I could not have brought out this book.

- - -

FOREWORD

Mr C. N. Nageswara Rao, whom I met first as a professional colleague, who later became a good friend, is a soft spoken, liberal and a cultured person with a deep urge to make this society a better place to live. I feel privileged to read his 'pearl string' of Tales carrying his humble messages to improve the society we live. His writing style is simple and direct. His Tales could be retold as bedtime stories, to illustrate values, long-walk conversation, and as good diversion in serious reading or talks.

The Tales speak of his respect for the self-less love of 'The Mother' and his preference for her emotional anchor over material wealth 'Partition'. The father in his tales teaches his son to experience 'Responsibility', bequeaths the 'Throne' but not the riches, and extols that the 'Conqueror' of the world may not necessarily be happy or at peace. He makes 'Son of the King' to walk away from the ordinary job.

The purpose of 'The Teacher' he believes is to transfer knowledge. The key to excel in studies is 'The Desire' to learn. Similarly unless one starts 'Living with the God' not being physically close at the temples or holy men, it is difficult to learn. In 'Sweetness of Labour', he emphasizes that efforts put in building a school makes the student satisfied more than from what he has learnt in the school. He looks at 'Criticism' as an opportunity to introspect. He wants all the students to know that goal is the great companion in 'Odyssey of Life'. He does not hesitate to make his 'Copy Cat' student to admit that some things cannot be copied.

The Tales speak that 'Talent' comes out of conviction, and 'Selection can be made through 'out of the box' thinking. Doing 'One at a Time' enables one to focus and be effective in his chosen field.

The Author does not mince his words in 'How We Look at It' between the well settled children abroad and those working before his eyes and the opportunity to cherish playing with the grand children. He knows that old age homes do not satisfy 'The Hunger for Love'.

The Author had carefully walked the razor's edge, while dealing contemporary social issues and managed to steer clear of subjectivity. Social order disrupted by arousing passions as in 'Rebellion', or the differences between "us and them" through 'Agitation' could only be restored by 'the King in the Palace' or 'the First in command', whose authority need to be respected for equity and fair play in society or the organizations. He emphasizes that 'The Tales of Heroes' motivate and that will of the individual 'Swayam Shakthi' makes for the invincible self.

It is not that the Tales could not have been better told, but the purpose of telling them places these tales on the pedestal much above the nuances of 'Grammar'.

The Author has set his tales in the villages, amongst the woods and trees, occasionally on the hilltops and palaces of the kings. His characters are the family members; yogis, saints and spiritual gurus; poets and musicians; the kings, the queens and the princes; the neighbourhood grocers, public servants and employees; the merchants, money lenders, the thieves and the dishonest that make readers to relate easily. The gods and the goddesses, demons and the ghosts; the birds and the animals make the stories colourful and interesting to the children.

I am sure these Tales will entertain the readers and will continue to be told and retold for a while; till the Author comes up with more beautiful and captivating further 'Tales'.

The Book should find its place in the school and public libraries and the houses of the parents yearning for responsible parenting.

I wish and eagerly await the next bouquet of Tales from the Author.

Sudhakar Rao Tenneti
Former Executive Director (HR),
Hindustan Aeronautics Limited, Bengaluru
16th October 2015

PREFACE

This book is a compendium of one hundred tiny tales. It is a treasure trove of timeless tales created to illumine young minds. It is a panoramic presentation on variegated glimpses of life captured from various standpoints.

Tales in this book are extremely tiny. They are shorter than short stories. But, pregnant with thought, they are titanic in their effect on human mind. They are crisp and clear. They are concise and concept based. They are ageless tales of all times, having no reference to any caste, creed, colour, country, region, religion, present or past. They are nameless and ageless. With universal appeal and transcending all geographical boundaries, they stand out as tales of the world and tales of all times.

The telling tales in this collection are written with a view to drive home thought stirring ideas that make readers think. They stand to play multifarious roles. They awaken, enlighten, educate and enchant readers. They mentor people to think differently and change their mindset for better. They motivate people to move from inaction to action. They dispel superstitions from minds and make minds clear to think freely. They, with stress on work philosophy in human life, highlight the need for seekers of success to take work as the only instrument of success. They, with philosophical touch and practical approach, make their mark on impressible minds of young readers, shape their outlook on human life and help in their personality development. Although the tales told are basically meant for the young and upcoming, they are equally applicable to elders, who need to read them to expand their horizon of thinking.

Tales included in this book provide for interesting, amusing and healthy reading for one and all. They help transit readers from narrow confines of living limited life to living larger life with holistic approach. They are purpose filled to kindle intellectual faculty in human mind. They envisage to make readers enlightened citizens of the world. Simple English is used in narration of the tales. It is earnestly hoped that this book will take readers on conducted tour of a literary world and delight them.

Author

INTRODUCTION

Ever since the art of communication developed in human history, telling tales has remained a favourite pastime for mankind. Right from its inception, tale has held sway over man. It has held its position as a source of great attraction. Whether it is what is told by mother to her children at bed time or told by raconteurs in close circles of chums or told by a seasoned story teller to convey a specific point with the objective of entertainment, enlightenment or education, it has a telling effect on mind. By size, it is Lilliputian. But by effect, it is Brobdingnagian. It is very impressive. It has got appeal for both mass as well as class. It has a wide ranging scope. It takes in its fold anything and everything in human life, right from a minute idea to something monumental in life.

There are many genres of expression in the field of literature. Out of all of them, tale is the oldest that has made way into human life and is the most popular. One main reason for why tale is the most sought after literary genre is its succinctness. Due to the brevity, people in the past have patronised it and people in the present are patronising it. Probably there is no other genre in literature that is as widely read as tale.

Tale is all pervasive. It is omnipresent. It not only exists independently by itself, but also finds its place in the midst of a long speech, narrative, novel or any other long drawn expression, in order to provide for relief to reader or listener from monotony. There is inseparable bonding between man and tale.

Although tale has remained a favourite of man from time immortal, it has become all the more so in the modern times. A modern man, breathlessly busy with his day to day occupational activities, is hardly finding time to read voluminous works. Like how many people have shifted their allegiance from filter coffee to instant coffee and test cricket to one day or T20 matches, modern readers, hard pressed for time, have switched over from reading long literary works to short literary works. In keeping with demand for short literary works, tale has undergone tremendous changes over a period of time and evolved into various variants to meet divergent demands of readers. Family tree of tale, as it stands today, is highly colossal, with a wide range of tales, starting from micro tales with very few words to macro tales with around ten thousand words, in its kitty.

Tales compiled in this book are extremely tiny, written keeping in view demand for short literary works, highly sought after by modern man. They are like loose snapshots arranged in a photo album that focus on glimpses of life. They are like independent framed portraits of great people, hung on walls in a hallowed hall of fame that stand to communicate in silence. They are written for a purpose. They are written to show wide angle view of life to readers and make them think. They are engaging, amusing and interesting.

Telling tales that find place in this book dwell on various topics of common interest. The topics are broad based. They encompass personal, family, social, professional, worldly, otherworldly, real, imaginary, routine, religious, spiritual, philosophical, success making, failure avoiding, life changing and many more issues that are relevant to the modern man in the context of strife torn modern society. Though they don't focus on any one subject specifically, they stand to highlight importance of hard work in life. Picked up from various walks of life and bunched together, they stand out as a bouquet of fragrant flowers that leave in a reader a pleasant smell to linger on in him for long.

It may be noted by readers that some Sanskrit words Mahayogi, meaning great follower of Yoga, Swayam Shakthi, meaning self is epitome of power and Vana, meaning forest, are deliberately used in some places of this book. Readers are also requested to note that certain abbreviations, used commonly in modern engineering industry, are used in this book.

It is expected that a trip through this book, with an itinerary full of one hundred sightseeing stopovers, will give readers an experience as wholesome as journey through life.

- - -

TELLING TALES

1. MOTHER

A godly man visited a village. He possessed super-natural powers. All villagers thronged to see him for fulfilment of their desires. An old woman went to see the man and stood before him with folded hands. The godly man said:

"Tell me mother, what can I do for you?"

"Bless me with long life," said the woman.

"Do you know how old you are?" said the godly man, taken aback.

"I know, I am past ninety years," said the woman.

"As it is, you are not keeping good health. Why do you want to live longer and suffer further," said the godly man.

"Bless me with long life. That is what I want from you," said the woman.

"Tell me one reason why you want to live long. If I am convinced, I shall make your wish come into reality," said the godly man.

"A saint predicted that my son would die soon after my death. I do not want my son to die," said the woman.

"I am told that your son has deserted you long ago, and you are all alone by yourself," said the godly man.

"What you heard is right. But still I want you to give me long life," said the woman.

"When your son has no concern for you, why do you show concern for him?" said the godly man.

"I am a mother," said the woman.

The godly man granted the boon that the mother desired to have.

- - -

2.   GUARANTEE

A rich man in a village had a son. The son was very queer. He did not do anything. The rich man persuaded his son to do something to come up in his life. But the son did not budge. The rich man was vexed. One day, he took his son to a saint and requested him to advise his son. The saint said to the son:

"What is the matter? Why are you not doing anything?"

"I don't like to do anything, because there is no guarantee that what I do will be a success. Unless it is guaranteed that what I do will be a success, I do not want to do anything," said the son.

"Will you do, if I give you the guarantee that whatever you do will be a success," said the saint.

"I shall joyfully do it," said the son.

"Then I shall do one thing. To give you the guarantee that you want, I shall propitiate god to invoke his blessings. Come and meet me after one month," said the saint.

The son along with his father went away and met the saint exactly after one month. The saint said:

"I have invoked blessings of the god. Whatever you will do henceforth will be a sure success. Start doing. For your success, I shall stand guarantee."

"If I don't succeed, what shall I do?" said the son.

"Punish me," said the saint, exuding confidence.

The son and his father went away. The son, after assurance from the saint, started doing something. He never got the opportunity to punish the saint.

- - -

3. AUSPICIOUS MOMENTS

There were two brothers in a family. The elder was learned. He knew how to refer to almanac and find out auspicious moments. He believed that doing anything on auspicious moments was sure to become a success. He did everything only on auspicious moments. On other than such moments, he never ventured to do anything.

The younger brother was more rational. He hardly believed in auspicious moments. He never postponed doing anything, waiting for auspicious moments. His did his works, right in time, depending on priority of the jobs.

Over passing of time, fortunes of the brothers changed significantly. The younger prospered in life and became very rich. The elder remained where he was at starting of his earning career. Once, a common friend of both the brothers asked the younger brother:

"Your brother does everything only on auspicious moments. In spite of it, he has not prospered in life. You don't do it. You have come up in life. Please tell me how it has happened."

"My brother does his works only on auspicious occasions, and most of the times, he does not do anything, because auspicious occasions occur very rarely. I do not see for auspicious moments to do my jobs and I keep doing most of the times. I have prospered in life, because I work most of the times and my brother has not prospered, because he works occasionally," said the younger brother.

- - -

4.   PREDICTION

Once, there lived a merchant who had immense faith in astrology. He was very curious to know about what was in store for him in future. He went to a famous astrologer, showed him his horoscope and requested him to forecast his future.

The astrologer went though the horoscope given by the merchant, studied the astral configurations and said:

"You are a very lucky man. Your stars are very good. They are in a benedictory mode. Take my word, whatever you will do will meet with instant success."

The merchant was very happy. He profusely thanked the astrologer for his prediction and returned. He waited for a few years for prediction of the astrologer to come true. But he found no change for better in his life. He remained as he was earlier. He became very wild with the astrologer. He went back to him and said:

"I am very unhappy with your prediction."

"What happened?" said the astrologer.

"What you have predicted has not come true," charged the merchant.

"What did I predict?" said the astrologer.

"You said that whatever I did was destined to meet with success," said the merchant.

"What did you do to get success?" said the astrologer.

The merchant realized his mistake, apologized to the astrologer and went back home. He started working. The astrologer's prediction came true.

- - -

5.   LIFE

Once, a merchant suffered losses in business. He went atop a hill to end his life. He saw a beautiful castle there. He went inside it. He found none, seen around anywhere there. He roamed all over the place for some time and reached assembly hall in top floor of the castle. He was surprised. He saw a king there, dressed gorgeously in his royal costume, sitting on a high placed throne and holding a meeting with his courtiers. The king noticed the merchant, invited him inside the court hall, offered him a seat to sit and said:

"What has brought you here?"

"I came here to end my life," said the merchant.

"Why do you want to end your life?" said the king.

"I am a very unlucky man. I have suffered losses in business," said the merchant.

"Do not end your life. You are not unlucky. You are luckier than me," said the king.

"With fabulous riches and a great castle to live in, how do you say that you are not lucky?" said the merchant.

"Because you are live and I am dead," said the king.

- - -

6.   NON-WALKER

Two walkers met regularly on a walkway. They were unknown to each other. One of them was a slow walker. He put his hands behind his back and walked very slowly. The other was very fast. He walked, as if he ran. One morning, the fast walker saw the slow walker walking slowly and steeped in deep thought. He thought that the slow walker did not know how to walk as a part of physical exercise. He wanted to educate the slow walker on how to walk. He met the slow walker, introduced himself and said:

"I wish to tell you something."

"Please tell me," said the slow walker.

"You are walking very slowly," said the fast walker.

"I know," said the slow walker.

"But that is not the way you have to walk. You must walk fast like me," said the fast walker.

"Why?" said the slow walker.

"Walking helps only if you walk fast, not if you walk slowly," said the fast walker.

"But who said that I am coming for walking," said the slow walker.

"I see you coming for a walk every day," said the fast walker.

"I don't come out to walk," said the slow walker.

"Then?" said the fast walker.

"I come out to think," said the slow walker.

- - -

7.   THE SECRET

Once, there lived a rich man in a village. He was opulently rich. He had no need to work. He ate well and led a very happy and leisurely way of life. Over years, he put on weight. His body became obese and became bulkier, day after day.

The rich man realized that it was time for him to reduce his weight. He consulted many for reduction of his weight. Someone told him to control intake of his diet. Someone told him to go for walking. Someone told him to go for physical workout. Someone told him to take medicines. The rich man tried all, but he could not reduce his weight. He remained as obese as he was. He was very sad at his plight.

One day, he went by bullock cart to his paddy field in outskirts of the village. He spent some time in the field and started back home. He felt thirsty. On the way, he saw an irrigation canal and a well nearby, at a distance from the road. Water in the canal was full. A washer man washed cloths on a slant stone slab on banks of the canal. His wife helped him by drying cloths on a rope tied to branches of a nearby banyan tree. The washer man and his wife worked hard under a hot and bright sun above.

The rich man wanted to go to the well, drink some water and quench his thirst. He asked driver of his cart to stop the cart. The cart man took the cart to a side and stopped it under shade of a tree. The rich man got down from the cart and went to the well. The cart man, who followed his master, drew out some water from the well and helped his master quench his thirst. The rich man was relieved. He went near the canal, where the washer man and his wife washed cloths. He grew very curious to talk to the couple, who deeply attracted his attention. He said to the washer man:

"You are working under hot sun. Don't you get tired?"

"No sir. I am used to this," said the washer man.

"You are very lean. What do you do to keep your body trim?" said the rich man.

The washer man blinked. He scratched his head and remained silent. The washer woman rushed to rescue of her husband. She said:

"He works."

- - -

8.   THE RECLUSE

A recluse lived all alone, in a cave dwelling on a hill in a forest. Tribal inhabitants in the forest attributed supernatural powers to the recluse and adored him like a living god.

One day, a hunter from a nearby hamlet desired to see the recluse in his cave. He was very innocent. He wanted to make some offerings to the recluse. He collected fruits, put them in a cane basket and took them to the recluse. The recluse greeted the hunter and said:

"What brings you here, my son?"

"I brought some fruits to offer to you," said the villager.

"Take them back," said the recluse.

"Why?" said the villager.

"I don't take them," said the recluse.

"Don't you take fruits?" said the villager.

"I don't take food," said the recluse.

"How can you work without taking food?" said the villager.

"I don't work," said the recluse.

"What for do you live, when you don't work?" said the villager.

The recluse drew blank. He had no answer. The hunter lifted up the basket on his head and returned. The recluse slipped into meditative mood.

After a few days, the villagers talked among themselves that the recluse had left his place. No one knew where he had gone.

- - -

9.   SOLUTION

Once, a man introspected and found out that he had many weaknesses in him. He felt very sorry for it. He wanted to get rid of the weaknesses in his personality. He thought of how to do it. He hit upon no clue. He decided to take help from an expert. He went to a famed mentor and told him his problem. The mentor said:

"Tell me what weaknesses you have got. I shall give my view on how to do away with the weaknesses."

"Don't ask me to tell what weaknesses I have got. I have many," said the man.

"But tell me what they are. Unless I know what they are, I can't offer a solution," said the mentor.

"You will be surprised, if I read out a list of them," said the man.

"Don't worry. That is my regular business. I hear problems from my clients and offer solutions for them," said the mentor.

"I want to remain cool always. But, many a time, I lose my cool and become very hot. I am very short tempered," said the man.

"Next," said the mentor.

"I don't want to give room for negative thoughts in my mind. But, unawares, I play host to negative thoughts," said the man.

"Next," said the mentor.

"I want to do things very fast. But I am not able to do so, because I am a perfectionist," said the man.

"Next," said the mentor.

"I want to do jobs, one after another. But I keep doing many jobs simultaneously and in the process I don't complete even a one, in time," said the man.

"Next," said the mentor.

"I can't tell you all. There are many, if I start telling you all," said the man.

"Yes. I can understand. You have many weaknesses," said the mentor.

"Please suggest how to remove weaknesses from my personality," said the man.

"I shall come back to you on that. But, before that tell me what strengths do you have," said the mentor.

"I don't know what strengths I have got. I have never looked out for them," said the man.

"Look out for strengths in you, not the weaknesses. That solves your problem," said the mentor.

- - -

10. BIRTH DAY

A boy developed queer curiosity to know how many great people were born on the day of a month, on which he was born. He collected details of the people, who were born on that day, from various sources that he could lay his hands on. He browsed through many sites in web to collect connected information on the subject. He did his job with serious obsession. He did it so, because he wanted to know whether he could become great in his life or not.

After the boy worked on the project for a long time, he concluded that no great man was born on the day that he was born on. He was distressed. He got into a depressive mood. He took it for granted that he too would not become great in his life, because there was no evidence of any great man having been born on that day.

One day, the boy sat in a melancholy mood in a forlorn spot. A sage that passed by saw the boy and said to him:

"You are very sad. What is the reason?"

"I find that no great man is born on the day, on which I am born."

"How do you say so?" crossed the sage.

"There is no evidence to confirm that a great man is ever born on the day that I am born on," said the boy.

"I can say very emphatically that your deduction is wrong," said the sage.

"Why do you say so?" said the boy.

"It is because one great man is born on that day," said the sage.

"Who is he?" said the boy.

"You," said the sage.

The boy cheered up. He rose from his seat with a lightened heart. He made up his mind to prove sagacious words of the sage right.

- - -

11. THE BOY AND SAINT

Once, a wandering saint saw a boy sitting in distress in premises of a temple and went to talk to him. He said to the boy:

"You are very sad. What is the matter?"

"I am very unlucky," said the boy.

"Why do you say so?" said the saint.

"I am not able to find a proper job for my livelihood," said the boy.

"Why do you say proper job? Did you try any job previously?" said the saint.

"I have tried many," said the boy.

"Tell me what you tried?" said the saint.

"I worked in fields. I could not fit in there. I worked in a grocery shop. I could not fit in there. After trying my luck in many areas, I came to the conclusion that I cannot fit in any field and eke out my livelihood," said the boy.

"How can you fit in mundane jobs, when you are cut out for something big?" said the saint.

"I don't understand you," said the boy.

"When you are born to become a king, how can you fit in jobs of insignificance?" said the saint.

"I fail to understand what you say, sir?" said the boy in amazement.

"What I say is right. You are destined to become a king. That is what I can make out from lines on your face. Do not settle down to doing common run works. Try. You will become a king," said the saint.

The boy got up and saluted the saint. The saint went away. The boy went his way to try what he was predicted to become. He did not fail in his effort. Prediction of the saint came true.

- - -

12.   SHOWCASING TALENT

A young artist had deep desire to showcase his histrionic talent on stage. He contacted a drama troupe and requested head of the troupe to give him a chance in the drama that they staged. The head tested calibre of the artist and found that he possessed good action talent, but it required further honing before being displayed on stage. He said the same to the artist. But the artist was not convinced. He prevailed upon the head to try him in his play. The head gave the youngster a chance. But the artist failed to prove his calibre on stage. He could not draw attention of public. He felt very sad. He doubted his own calibre. He left the drama troupe and went away. He could not understand where he went wrong.

The artist set out on a long tour. One day, he happened to pass by outskirts of a village, under hot sun. He was tired. He looked out for a tree under which he could rest for a while. He saw a thatched hut nearby, with a big tree beside it, casting shade all around. He went to the tree and sat under cool shade of it. He saw a sculptor in front of the thatched hut. There lay stocked nearby the hut many raw stones yet to be sculpted by the sculptor. The artist grew curious to go near the hut and see the stones. He went to the hut. The sculptor, who moved around outside the hut, greeted the artist warmly. The artist introduced himself as a wayfarer and said to the sculptor:

"Are you a sculptor?"

"Yes," said the sculptor.

"What do you make?" said the artist.

"I make idols of deities," said the sculptor.

"Are you presently working on any idol?" said the artist.

"Of course," said the sculptor.

"May I see some idols made by you," said the artist.

"You are welcome to do so," said the sculptor.

The sculptor took the artist inside the hut and showed him some finished idols arranged neatly in racks in a corner. The artist saw the idols with ecstasy and praised craftsmanship of the sculptor. He saw a huge thing covered with a cloth in middle of the house. The artist grew curious to see it and said to the sculptor:

"What is this?"

"It is also idol of a deity," said the sculptor.

"Why did you cover it with a cloth?" said the artist.

"It is not yet finished," said the sculptor.

"Can I not have a look at it," said the artist.

"I am sorry. I can't allow you to see it," said the sculptor.

"Why?" said the artist.

"I showcase what I want to showcase only when it is finished in all respects and there is nothing more for me to do on it. Until then I can' show what I want to show to others," said the sculptor.

The artist got answer for where he went wrong in showcasing of his talent. He thanked the sculptor and left the place, abruptly. He went into oblivion for some time, prepared himself for a big show, re-entered the theatrical stage with a big bang and blasted off to success.

- - -

13. OPINIONS VARY

There lived two merchants in a town. One day, one merchant met another merchant in his shop and said to him:

"I want a small feedback from you."

"Tell me," said the second merchant.

"A boy that has worked with you until a week ago wants to join my shop. What is your opinion about him?" said the first merchant.

"He is very sincere and committed. You may employ him, if you want," said the second merchant.

"I am surprised with your feedback," said the first merchant.

"Why," said the second merchant.

"I never expected this feedback from you," said the first merchant.

"Why do you say so," said the second merchant.

"What the boy has told me about you is that you are not good," said the first merchant.

"Let the boy have any opinion about me. But my opinion about the boy is he is good and he may be employed," said the second merchant.

The first merchant thanked the second merchant and went his way.

- - -

14. DOING A JOB

A voyager traversed a good part of the world, underwent many experiences and returned home after many years. He earned sufficiently. He took a serious resolve not to venture out any more and face troubles. He decided to be at home for rest of his life. He turned to spending his days happily in the company of his family members. Days passed off peacefully.

After a few days, the voyager felt that he was wasting away his time. It occurred to him that he could draw on his lifelong experiences and write a book based on them. The very idea electrified him. The voyager swung into action immediately. He embarked upon writing a travelogue.

He undertook the job with serious commitment. He drew out material required for the book from archives of his memory, made a layout and set himself on writing. In the beginning, he thought that he could finish his work in a few months. But, as things went on, he perceived that there was no commendable progress in his work. He proceeded at snail's pace. However hard he tried to speed up his work, he could not make any headway. He was beset with many problems. Every day, he planned to finish part of the task on hand. But, every day, he failed to complete it. He analyzed why he was not able to do what he planned. He realized that many family related problems and emergency works that he never foresaw stood as stumbling blocks in what he took up to do.

When he could not make progress in his work even after a few years, he grew highly desperate. He doubted if at all he could finish his work. He went to a saint to clarify his doubt. The saint heard the voyager and said to him:

"How determined are you to finish the work that you have taken up?"

"I am very much determined," said the voyager.

"Do one thing. Give up writing the book. You can never finish it," said the saint.

"Why do you say so?" said the voyager, taken aback.

"Of many jobs that are on your hand, you are according least importance to writing book," said the saint.

"No. I am giving topmost priority for it," said the voyager emphatically.

"You have time to attend to your family problems. You have time to attend to emergency works. You have time to do everything on earth. But you hardly find time to get going with writing the book. And you say that you are according topmost priority for writing your book," said the saint.

What the saint meant went into head of the voyager. The voyager realized his mistake, made obeisance to the saint and took leave of him. He changed his way of working. He withdrew himself from all mundane activities, retired to a place far away from home, concentrated on his creative work and finished it very soon.

- - -

15.   REVELATION

There lived a businessman in a town. He was always busy with his business activities. He started from home right in the morning and reached back home only late in the night. He hardly found time to do anything other than looking after his business related matters.

One day, a religious speaker came to the town. Devout followers of the speaker organised a speech by the speaker in a big auditorium in the town. Invitation came to the businessman to attend to the speech. The businessman, prevailed upon by his fellow businessmen, went to the auditorium to attend to the speech. The speech was attended by a huge congregation of devotees. The speaker addressed the gathering and delivered a speech on life and death and said at the end:

"Remember that you are a guest on earth. You have not come to stay here permanently. You will have to vacate your place to someone else at some point of time or other. Span of your life is very short. Do what we want to do in life, before life draws to an end. Death is right in front of you, well in threshold of your house. It can tap at door of your house, anytime. Be prepared to face it."

The businessman found it very hard to digest speech of the speaker. It appeared to him as if the speech was well directed at him. He returned home, highly disturbed and gripped in gloom.

Wife of the businessman was at loss to understand why her husband turned gloomy, all of a sudden. She tried to elicit truth from her husband. But, the businessman maintained stoic silence. The thought of death constantly smote the businessman. Ultimately, it told upon his health. The businessman fell ill.

Many doctors attended on the businessman. But no one could establish reason for his illness. The businessman continued to be on bed. One day, he called his wife and said to her:

"I may not live long. After me, take care of the family."

Wife of the businessman was a shrewd lady. She understood that her husband suffered not from physical illness, but from some unknown worry. She wanted to know about it and said:

"What on earth makes you think that you will not live long?"

The businessman hesitated for a while and revealed to his wife what the religious leader said. Wife of the businessman said:

"There is nothing new about it. Death will come to everyone, one day."

"You don't know. Death is right in front of me," said the businessman.

"Will it come this instant, if you call it?" said wife of the businessman.

"No," said the businessman.

"Can you resist it, if it comes right now?" said wife of the businessman.

"No," said the businessman.

"When you have no control over it, leave it to itself. Let it come, whenever it wants to come. Don't wait for it. You are not sure of when it will come. Until it comes, do whatever you want to do. You have better business with life than death," said wife of the businessman.

Something in what his wife said appealed to the businessman. The businessman cheered up. His eyes sparkled. He sat up on bed, shook off fear of death that possessed him like a ghost and got up. His mind became light with thought of death deleted from it. It did not take long for him to convalesce and return to active life in his business. Wife of the businessman succeeded in making her husband think differently and come out of fear of death that gripped him.

- - -

16. GODDESS

Once, a man developed a wrong desire for something. He got infatuated with it. He felt that he could not live without it. He fondly wished for materialization of it. He heard that the deity presiding over a temple in his village was very powerful and she would help realize desires of her devotees. He went to the temple and offered prayers to the deity, very devoutly.

Days, weeks, months and years passed. The man continued his prayers with no letup. But the deity did not appear before the man and bestow upon him the boon that he wanted. At long last, the man lost his temper. He stood before idol of the deity and chided her. The deity appeared before the man in human form and said:

"Why are you chiding me for all the goodness that I have caused to you?"

"What goodness did you cause to me?" said the man.

"I have seen to it that your wish did not materialize," said the deity.

"But I prayed for materialization of it," said the man.

"And I did not make your wish come through," said the deity.

"But why?" said the man.

"Because, I am a goddess," said the deity.

- - -

17.   UNIQUE BOY

A boy read stories of many great men. Whenever he read the story of a great man, he got deeply influenced by him and tried to become as great as the great man, in his own way. It continued until he read the story of another great man and tried to copy the second great man. Years passed. Even though the boy tried to copy many great men, he could not become like any one of them. He became despondent.

One day, he met a diviner and poured out to him what was there in his mind. The diviner heard the boy coolly and said to him:

"Of all, why do you want to become like others?"

"Because they are great," said the boy.

"But you are not like them," said the diviner.

"Can I not become great like others?" said the boy.

"Why you cannot become? You can become greater than them," said the diviner.

"I don't believe you," said the boy.

"Believe me. What I say is true. You are unimaginably great. None like you has ever taken birth in the past and none like you will ever take birth in the future. You are highly unique. There is none in the world comparable to you. Stop copying to become what others have already become. Start striving to become what you can become by yourself. Mark my words. You are set to surpass all others, if you wish. Rise high to touch sky as limit. Come back to report, if I am wrong," said the diviner.

The boy did not go back to the diviner to prove him wrong.

- - -

18. TALES OF HEROES

A mother of two children was a highly enlightened lady. Whenever she got a chance, she told her children tales of national heroes, heroes from folklore, epics, history and her own world of imagination. She narrated the tales, told her children to note how the heroes attained stardom and asked them to emulate their examples to become as great as the heroes.

Father of the children was a man of different stuff. He was highly professional. He disapproved of what his wife did. He believed that teaching of sciences, mathematics, languages and other subjects was of more practical relevance than telling tales of heroes to his children.

One day, the wife narrated, at bed time, tale of a super hero from an epic that performed many supernatural and stupendous works in his life time. Children listened to her with keen interest and slowly slipped into sleep. The husband said to his wife:

"You are a learned lady. Why don't you teach the children sciences, mathematics and other subjects that are of more use to them? Spinning yarns will not take them anywhere."

"I need not teach school subjects at home," said the wife.

"Why do you say so?" said the husband.

"There is a school to teach them the subjects," said the wife.

"What is the use of telling tales of heroes to the children," said the husband.

"To help them become heroes in their lives," said the wife.

- - -

19. MAHAYOGI

An old man, who lived in the company of saints and sages in the Himalayas, learnt yoga and became a yogi. He understood that yoga acted like a panacea for many physical and mental ailments suffered by householders. He wanted to part with his knowledge to the aspirants that needed his help. He returned to the city from which he hailed, opened a yoga centre for practising of yoga and taught techniques of the art to the needy that visited his centre. Over the years, he became very famous and many people became his disciples. Now and then, the yogi, along with his followers, went on visits to neighbouring villages and educated people in the field of yoga.

One day, the yogi received invitation from headman of a remote village to visit his place. The yogi, along with one of his disciples, set out on a journey on foot to the village. On the way, he happened to pass by a field, in which a farmer worked on a pulley operated bucket system that helped draw out water from a well and irrigated his field. The yogi and his disciple were thirsty. They went to the well, where the farmer worked, drank handfuls of water and retired to a sideway to rest for a while. The farmer stopped his work for a while, went to a nearby hut, brought some fruits, offered them to the yogi and his disciple and went back to his work. The disciple felt very happy with courtesy meted out by the farmer. He said to the yogi:

"The farmer is very courteous. He has treated us very kindly. We need to give him something in return."

"What can we give him?" said the Yogi.

"Shall we teach this farmer how to practise yoga?"

"No," said the yogi.

"Why?" said the disciple.

"He is a mahayogi," said the yogi.

- - -

20.   NEIGHBOURHOOD

A man living in a locality got disenchanted with his neighbourhood. He developed a feeling that his neighbours were not good. He remembered various incidents that occurred in the past and felt for sure that his neighbours were not cooperative and he had a tiff with many of them over some or other issue. He was deeply hurt. He concluded that a man like him could not stay in a locality that was unfriendly with him. He thought and thought on how to handle the situation, found no way out, decided to sell his house and move away to a new locality where better people lived. He made enquiries for better places of living and chose a new locality where he could move to. He put up his house for sale. A prospective seller met him, introduced himself and said:

"Sir, I understand that your house is for sale. I want to buy it."

"Please do so. You will like this house," said the seller.

"Thank you, sir" said the buyer.

"How do you propose to pay for the property?" said the seller.

"I have a house of my own in a different locale of city. I want to sell it and buy this property from sale proceeds of it," said the buyer.

"Where are you put up presently?" said the seller.

"In Hill Shire," said the buyer.

"That is one of the best locales in the city, where most polished people are known to stay. Why do you want to sell your house there?" said the seller.

"Oh! Don't talk about people staying in my locality. The people are very uncultured and quarrelsome," said the buyer.

"What you say is breaking news for me. All along, I am under the impression that people of Hill Shire are very good. In fact I like the place so much that I want to buy a property there and settle in the place permanently," said the seller.

"I am so much fed up with people in my locality that I want to sell my property for whatever offer I get and get out of the place as early as possible. From this, you may understand how bad people in my locality are," said the buyer.

"Thank you for your feedback," said the seller.

"It is fine. Shall we talk about our sale transaction, now?" said the buyer.

"I don't want to sell my house," said the seller.

- - -

21. DEVILS ON TREE

A man was highly selfish. He was cunning. He came up in life at the cost of many others. He operated with sole motto of furthering his selfish interests and crushed ruthlessly many people that came in his way. He was draconian. He was dreaded by one and all. He did many types of undesirable jobs and rose so high in his life that others could not even dream to reach him. Still, he was not satisfied with his growth. He continued to try hard and hard to climb up to newer heights.

One day, the man happened to go into forest. He was all alone in the place. He lost his way back home. He wandered for a long time and reached a lake, beside which there stood a big tree. There were many souls hanging onto branches of the tree. At sight of the man, a soul quickly descended from the tree, approached him and said very politely:

"I welcome you. There is a place reserved for you on the tree."

"Who are you?" said the man.

"I am a permanent resident of this place. I am designated to welcome new comers," said the soul.

"How do you know that I am coming to this place?" said the man.

"We are clairvoyant. We know who is set to come here. We know very well that you will come here, one day," said the soul.

"It is a real wonder. I am amazed at your power of clairvoyance. It is really great of you that you have foreseen my coming here and reserved a place for me on the tree," said the man.

"That is how we take care of people of our class," said the soul.

"Which class do you belong to?" said the man.

"The class of devils," said the soul.

The man shuddered at what the devil said. He shrieked, stirred and sat up on bed, on which he slept. It took some time for him to realize that he had a dream, a devil spoke to him in the dream and a place was reserved for him on the tree on which devils dwelt. He had enough sense to understand why he had a dream of that sort. He changed himself and lived life of a good man, thereafter.

- - -

22.   KING AND HIS SON

A king founded a kingdom and ruled it for a very long time. He became old. He decided to step down and hand over the throne to his son. Before he did so, he wanted to richly reward all the courtiers in his court that stood by him during his long rule. He called for a meeting of all the courtiers, whom he wanted to reward. The courtiers assembled in the court hall. The king addressed the courtiers one by one, remembered the services that they had rendered during their service, extolled their virtues and rewarded them richly. He divided his kingdom into various divisions and made the courtiers lords of the divisions, one each.

The son of the king, who was present in court during the event, was dejected. He was not happy. He could not digest what his father did. He suppressed his feelings with great difficulty and remained silent. After the court meet was over and all courtiers left the court hall, the prince said to the king:

"You distributed the entire kingdom among our courtiers. What am I left with now?"

"The throne," said the king.

- - -

23.   THE SON OF A KING

A king lost his war and died on battlefield. His queen escaped with her young son from fort, fled to a remote village far away from capital of the kingdom and lived in a thatched hut with her identity not revealed to anyone.

Son of the prince grew in the village atmosphere. He joined a small school and learnt something that could support his life in the days to come. By the time he finished studies in the school, he attained age of a young man and maturity dawned on him. He decided to search for a job somewhere and eke out a living. He went to a nearby town, met a mill owner and said to him:

"Will you be pleased to offer a job for me in your mill?"

"Who are you?" said the mill owner.

"I am son of a king," said the young man.

"I don't believe your words," said the mill owner.

"I swear on my words," said the young man.

"Prove that you are son of a king," said the mill owner.

The young man turned away from the mill owner to prove that he was son of a king. He proved himself to be not only son of a king, but also a king by himself.

- - -

24. DEATH AFTER ONE YEAR

Once, a man wandered aimlessly in a forest. He was very sad and crestfallen. He appeared as if a big load was on his head and he was not able to carry it. A travelling saint met the man on way and greeted him:

"You are very sad. What is the matter?'

The man did not reply. He started crying. The saint consoled him and said:

"Tell me. What is the matter? If I can help you, I shall help you."

"What can I tell you about me? I am an unlucky man," said the man.

"Tell me the reason. Why do you think so?" said the saint.

"I have come to know that I am going to die after one year," said the man.

"Who has said it?" said the saint.

"A diviner saw my horoscope and predicted," said the man.

"Is it the only cause of your concern?" said the saint.

"Can there be any other reason that can make a man sad?" said the man.

"If that is the reason that makes you sad, I feel that you should not become sad, but become cheerful," said the saint.

"Why do you say so?" said the man.

"You are sure to live for one year. Is it not consoling?" said the saint.

"But I am going to live only for one year," said the man.

"Be happy. You have assurance that you will live for one year. That assurance is not there for me. With no such assurance, how sad should I feel?" said the saint.

The man saw other side of the coin. He got relieved. He buoyed up. He thanked the saint and went away his way.

- - -

25. HOW WE LOOK AT IT

Two childhood friends met in a hill top fair, after a long time. They were excited to see each other, after nearly five decades. They shook hands, hugged each other, exchanged pleasantries, remembered their good old days and retired to sideways for a relaxed talk.

"How are you?" said the first friend.

"I am very happy. I was working for a company earlier. One year ago, I have superannuated from my service. Now I am at home. I have three children. All are well educated. They are married and have gone to foreign lands. They send me money every now and then. I am extremely happy, leading a happy and peaceful retired life along with my wife. I feel elated to think that all my children are well settled abroad," said second friend.

"It is very nice to hear that all your children have come up in life and they are happy abroad," said first friend.

"How about you?" said second friend.

"I am extremely happy. I am in the line of agriculture. I have two sons. Both are married and well settled. They stay with me in my house. They help me in my field work. I feel thrilled to see my children and grand children right in front of my eyes," said first friend.

- - -

26. DESIRE

A teacher ran a primary school in street side veranda of his tiled house. He taught students that hailed from neighbouring localities. He thrived on whatever little he received from his students.

Everyday, when he taught in class, he noticed that a young boy loitered around in street around his house and looked curiously at how he taught in his class room. He wondered who the boy could be. He wanted to ask the boy about who he was. But he refrained from it, because he did not want to hurt feelings of the boy. Although he saw the boy regularly, he feigned as if he did not notice him. Days passed.

One evening, after the school was over, when the teacher was about to pack up for the day, he noticed the boy passing by his house and casting glances at him. He called the boy and said:

"Who are you?"

"I am the son of a labourer staying in a slum nearby," said the boy, with reflection of fear in his tone.

"What is making you loiter around here and glare at us?" said the teacher.

"I feel happy to watch when you teach and your students learn," said the boy.

"Don't you go to school?" said the teacher.

"I don't," said the boy.

"Why?" said the teacher.

"I work in a shop for daily wages. I cannot afford to go to school," said the boy.

"Do you want to learn, if I teach you in my leisure hours?" said the teacher.

"But I cannot pay you," said the boy.

"Don't pay me. I shall teach you, free of charge," said the teacher.

"I shall be very happy to learn, if you teach me freely," said the boy.

The teacher noticed that there was deep desire in the boy to learn. He initiated the boy into studies and started teaching him basics. The boy applied himself to studies and rose very fast to expectations of his teacher. The teacher was very happy with progress made by his student. He made the boy stop going to the shop, where he worked, arranged free boarding and lodging for him in his house and put him on dedicated studies. The boy proved his mettle. He excelled in studies and became highly knowledgeable. A burning desire to learn made the boy win laurels.

- - -

27. RESPONSIBILITY

A cart maker made carts in a village. He made a variety of carts to suit to various applications of villagers. He worked hard, established himself in his field and earned handsomely.

He was a happy man, save for his son. His son, late in his teens, did nothing for livelihood. He moved freely with his friends and whiled away time. The cart man persuaded and prevailed upon his son to help support him in his business. But the son did not heed. He showed no interest in business of his father.

One day, the cart man received an order for ten new carts from a local lord. It was said to him that the carts were to be made ready within one month and the deadline was not to be missed. The cart man knew that the local lord was very authoritative and he would not take it lightly, if his order was not executed in time. He took the order as a blessing in disguise. He wanted to leverage it for his advantage. He called his son and said:

"I am going on a pilgrimage trip along with your mother. Will you take care of our workshop, until I come back?"

"How long is your trip?" said the son.

"About a month," said the cart maker.

"Make sure that you will come back in time," said the son, consenting for his father's proposal, half heartedly.

"That I shall do," said the cart maker.

The cart maker briefed his son on order received from the local lord and other pending works in the workshop, left his workshop in the hands of his son and set out with his wife on his pilgrimage trip. He returned only after six months.

He found no need to go back to his workshop. His son managed it very well.

- - -

28.   COMPOSER OF MUSIC

Once, a king happened to stay in a village for a few days. During his stay, he chanced upon a farmer-poet, who composed very good lyrics. He took fancy for compositions of the poet. He spoke to the poet, took him to his capital, made him a court poet and asked him to work on his creative activity with total dedication. He liked compositions of the poet so much that he made it a practice to listen to songs of the poet regularly. He encouraged the poet to write new songs and please him.

The poet in court of the king was very happy. He enjoyed all material comforts provided by the king and worked with dedication to create new lyrics in music. Things went on very well for a few days. After some time, the king noticed that the poet did not compose his new works as beautifully as he did before coming to the court. He wondered how it happened. Out of courtesy, he did not open out his mind to the poet. But he felt that the poet did not deserve to continue in the court. He consulted his chief minister and took a decision. He called for a court meet and honoured the poet publicly in presence of all courtiers. He said to the poet:

"We are honoured to honour you for great lyrics composed by you. We are very happy to gift you with a large chunk of farm land in your village. You may go to your village and cultivate it."

The poet was pleased with magnanimity of the king. He left the court, went to his village, took possession of the land allocated to him and cultivated it. In the process, he fell back into his groove. He started composing excellent musical works again. On invitation by the king, he went to court, every now and then, and pleased connoisseurs of music with his works. The king connived to draw out real worth from the poet.

- - -

29. SELECTION

The owner of a production company wanted to expand his business operations manifold. He called for a high level meet of group heads of his company, opened out his mind to them and asked what they wanted to implement what he proposed. The group heads projected requirement of additional manpower. The owner agreed to provide additional manpower. He asked heads of Management Services Department and Human Resources Department to collect man power requirements of individual departments, consolidate the same and put up to him for further action. MSD and HRD worked jointly on the project. They compiled a list and saw the owner with the list. The owner went through the list and said to them:

"The requirement is pretty large. How shall we go about the recruitment?"

"As per practice in vogue in the company," said HRD Head.

"What is the practice?" said the owner.

"Advertising for recruitment, conducting written examination for preliminary screening and making final selection through viva-voce," said HRD Head.

"Is it not a long drawn process?" said the owner.

"Yes, it is," said HRD Head.

"Why we should not try a new line of recruitment?" said the owner.

"May we know what it is," said the HRD Head.

"Pick up toppers from all academic institutions in and around our company," said the owner.

"Toppers of all institutions may not be of the same standard," said HRD Head.

"That they have topped in their respective institutions speaks volumes for their worth. Let us try this and see if we can get better man power," said the owner.

The HRD Head tried the new way of recruitment. He was more than satisfied with quality of man power that he got.

- - -

30. VISIT TO HOME TOWN

A man, hailing from a poor family, grew up in middle class locality of a small town. He studied well, rose in life, migrated to a far off city, started a business, expanded it and established himself as a big man, in his new place of settlement. He was very nostalgic. He often recalled in what circumstances he grew up in his childhood, how his mother struggled to bring him up, how people in neighbourhood of his house supported him and his mother, the friends he moved with, the places that he frequented and each and everything that connected him to his place of birth.

Whenever someone came to see him from his place of birth, he enquired warmly how the people that he knew about were and felt very happy to know that people in his home town still remembered him and talked about him. Many a time, he thought of going to his home town, see all the people that he left long ago, help people that were in need and donate liberally for the school, where he studied. But his wish never materialized. Every time that he thought of going to his home town, he was forced to postpone it, because of his busy schedule of life and inescapable preoccupations.

At long last, after many years, he extricated himself from his busy schedule and went to his home town to see, meet and talk to all people that he was acquainted with. He went to the locality where he spent his childhood and looked out for the people whom he knew. He found to his utter dismay that he came across no acquaintance. On enquiry, he came to know that the people whom he asked for went into oblivion long ago. There was hardly anyone whom he could recognise or who recognised him. His desire to see the people of his acquaintance did not materialise. He visited places, with no people that he knew, with a heavy heart and returned home, downhearted. He rued, he should have visited his home town when people that he knew were still alive.

- - -

31.   SEVEN DEITIES

There lived seven deities in separate shrines dedicated to them, at foot of a hill inside a deep forest. Forest dwellers worshipped them regularly with prayers and offerings and held fairs in the name of them, at different times of a year. The deities enjoyed worshipping by the tribal devotees and lived blissfully in their places, for ages on end.

As times changed, forest lands thinned out and many dwellers in forest moved away into folds of new occupations. The youngsters did not offer prayers to the seven deities as devoutly as their forefathers. The deities felt sorry for the change in attitude of the native devotees.

The youngest of the deities could not compromise with decline in devotion of her devotees. She wanted to kindle devotion in devotees towards her. She possessed a priest and made him utter in public that a big catastrophe would befall the devotees, if they did not offer prayers to her regularly. The devotees were afraid. They made arrangements to pray to the youngest deity with all religious rituals.

The second youngest of the deities took cue from what her youngest sister did and followed suit. The tribal people started offering prayers to her too. The other sisters, excepting the eldest, followed suit and succeeded to get prayers from their devotees. The eldest of the deities did nothing to make her devotees pray to her. She kept quiet. One day, the six sisters met their eldest sister and proposed:

"Do what we have done to make devotees pray to you."

"I do not want to do anything of that sort," said the eldest deity.

"Why?" said the six deities.

"I want to remain a god," said the eldest deity.

- - -

32. BELIEF IN GOD

A young priest worked in a temple. Every day, after evening prayers in the temple, he met devotees and heard them tell their woes. He offered to them solutions that he deemed right and tried to give them solace. He said to every devotee:

"Do not worry. The god is there with you. He will help solve your problems. Have belief in Him."

Over the years, the priest observed that there was a steep fall in number of devotees that visited to discuss their problems with him. He wondered why a sudden change came over the devotees. On enquiry, he found that devotees, instead of coming to him, went to an old priest in a different temple to pour out their problems before him. He grew curious to know what the old priest did to satisfy his devotees. He went to the old priest to observe what he did. He was stunned with what he saw. The old priest did exactly what he did. He waited until all devotes left the temple, introduced himself and said to the old priest:

"Sir, you are telling devotees exactly the same what I am telling. Devotees are satisfied with you and not satisfied with me. May I know where I am failing to satisfy my devotees?"

"You are saying to your devotees that 'god is there with you'," said the old priest.

"You too are saying the same thing," said the young priest.

"I am doing something more than that," said the old priest.

"What is it?" said the young priest.

"I am invoking god to make Him dwell in the devotees," said the old priest.

"Why?" said the young priest.

"When you say that 'god is there with you', devotees may or may not believe that god is there with them. But when I perform a ritual to invoke god and make Him dwell in the devotees, the devotees believe that god has entered them and He is there with them. The devotees are coming to me, because I am making the god dwell in them," said the old priest.

- - -

33.   CLAIRVOYANT MAN

A predictor possessed clairvoyant skills. He interacted with people, read their minds and predicted very accurately what they would become in their lives. People revered him as a godly man.

One day, an astrologer, who developed high respect for the predictor, met him and said:

"You are very great, sir."

"Why?" said the predictor.

"What you are predicting is coming out to be exactly true," said the astrologer.

"I am happy to hear it," said the predictor.

"I want to know whether you are following astrology, palmistry, numerology or some other method for your predictions," said the astrologer.

"I follow no one of them," said the predictor.

"If it is so, I want to know how you are predicting?" said the astrologer.

"I interact with a person on a number of occasions and predict what he will become in his life," said the predictor.

"What do you get to know from the interaction?" said the astrologer.

"What the man wishes to become in his life," said the predictor.

"To get to know what the man wishes to become in his life, where is the need for you to talk to a person, again and again, at different points of time?" said the astrologer.

"To make sure that the man is with the same wish all throughout," said the predictor.

"How does it help you predict?" said the astrologer.

"If a man is living with what he wants to become in life consistently all throughout, he is sure to become what he wants to become in life," said the predictor.

- - -

34.   A WISE MERCHANT

There lived a merchant in a town. He ran a grocery shop in a busy market place. He had a grown up son. The son did nothing worthwhile. He took money from home and spent it away with his friends. The merchant tried very hard to change his son. But when his efforts bore no fruit, he devised a plan. He started a new grocery shop in a different part of town and asked his son to run it. The son resisted the move. But the merchant did not relent. The disgruntled son took up the job reluctantly.

The shop run by the son incurred losses. The son proposed to close the shop on account of incurring losses. But the merchant did not agree. He pumped new funds into business of the new shop and compensated for the losses. This happened recurrently, many a time. Every time, the merchant did the same. The merchant's wife was exasperated. One day, she said to the merchant:

"You are supporting a business that is unsustainable."

"I know it," said the merchant.

"Why don't you close down the business that is running into frequent losses?" said the merchant's wife.

"I don't want to do it," said the merchant.

"Why?" said the merchant's wife.

"My son in business is more profitable to me than when he is not in business," said the merchant.

"What do you mean??" retorted the merchant's wife.

"The investment that I make on my son sustains him long when he is in business than when he is not in business,"

"Why do you say so?" said the merchant's wife.

"Business brings in returns. My son does not," said the merchant.

- - -

35. THE TREE

An old woman installed wooden idol of a deity under a huge banyan tree and offered prayers to the deity regularly. The tree with a massive hood of leaves, big trunk and many overhanging roots cast cool shade and created ideal location for the deity. Many local people and long distance wayfarers, who passed by a way nearby, came to the tree and offered their prayers to the deity. The old woman, who dwelt in a makeshift dwelling at back of the tree, played the role of a priestess and lived on offerings made by devotees.

The old woman grew older. Her grandson took over her job. The young man was not happy with set up under the tree. He decided to build a shrine for the deity. He collected donations from donors, felled the tree that came in the way of construction of the shrine and built a shrine for the deity. He engaged a pundit and made arrangements for offering of prayers to the deity, more regularly and ritualistically. But he was disappointed. He noticed to his surprise that there was steep fall in number of devotees that visited the shrine. He did not understand where he went wrong and developed a doubt if he did something to displease the deity. He asked his grandmother:

"There is sudden dip in number of devotees visiting the shrine. It never happened previously. What could be the reason?"

"Devotees come to pray to goddess. But where is the goddess to pray to?" said the grandmother.

"What do you mean? The goddess is very much there in the shrine," said the grandson.

"How do you say so?" said the grandmother.

"The idol that stands for the goddess is there in the shrine," said the grandson.

"But the goddess is not there in the idol," said the grandmother.

"Where is it?" said the grandson.

"It is there in the tree that you felled," said the grandmother.

The grandson realized his mistake and corrected it. He grew not only one tree but many trees in close proximity of the shrine and brought back sanctity and serenity to the spot. The place became holy again. The deity returned to her erstwhile place of stay. Devotees followed suit.

- - -

36.   MAN ON HILL

A man stood on peak of a tall hill. He noticed a young lad at foot of the hill. The lad looked at the man keenly. The man grew curious to know why the lad stared at him. He said aloud:

"Why are you staring at me?"

"I am seeing that you are on peak of the hill," said the lad.

"So I am," said the man.

"How did you go up?" said the lad.

"I climbed up the hill," said the man.

"Can I come up the hill?" said the lad.

"You may do so," said the man.

"How can I come up?" said the lad.

"The way I have come up," said the man.

The lad made a way, climbed up and stood on peak of the hill.

- - -

37. FEAR

A group of employees met daily in a bar. They drank, ate, chatted and spent happy times, until late in nights. They shared bar charges, turn by turn. Years passed. The employees turned old. But, they continued their die hard habit with no letup.

Things took a turn, all of a sudden. One of the group members fell ill and died. The incident had its effect on other members. For some mystic reason, other members of the group, excepting one, died one after another, in a quick succession. The last man got panicky. He was crestfallen. He developed fear that he too would go very soon. He became sickly. He went to a doctor for general check up. The doctor conducted all types of medical tests and confirmed that the man was fully healthy and there was no problem for him from health point of view. But the fear that all of his friends left him and he too would go very soon haunted the man.

And one fine morning, he died, all of a sudden.

- - -

38. FILM ACTOR

A talented film actor suddenly ran out of roles in films. Film producers that queued up to take him into their films, earlier, shied away from him. No one of them gave him a chance to act in his films. The actor did not understand why the film industry put him aside. He felt bad. He wanted to know what reason for sudden change in people in film industry towards him was. He went to a music director, who was a good friend of him, and shared his feelings with him. The music director was busy. He was on his way to a film studio. He took the actor along with him to the studio and made him sit beside him.

Shooting was about to start in the set. A senior actor was in his place, ready to play his role in a scene. The film director stood on a side and issued instructions to the actor. Shooting started. The actor acted. The action was superb. But the director was not satisfied. He told the actor to change his action and perform again. The actor did not complain. He complied with instruction of the director and performed again. The first performance of the actor was better than second performance. But the director approved of the second performance and moved to the next shot. The talented actor was stunned. He said to his friend:

"Don't you think that direction of the director is not up to mark?"

"Why do you say so?" said the music director.

"First performance of the actor is far better than his second performance. But the director has chosen the second one," said the actor.

"That is the reason why you have run out of roles," said the music director.

"What do you mean?" said the actor.

"Never question judgement of director. How to direct is his prerogative. When you act, learn to listen to what the director says. Otherwise, what happens is what has happened to you," said the music director.

The actor learnt to play the role that he was supposed to play and not the role that someone else was supposed to play.

- - -

39.   LIVING WITH GOD

A student was very devout. He went to temple every day and offered prayers to god. One night, when he went to temple, there was a religious congregation on in assembly hall of the temple complex. He joined the congregation. A saintly man delivered speech on god:

"Most of us do not know how to come up in life. We are always in a state of confusion as to what to do and what not to do to rise in life. God, in his many manifestations, has solutions for our intriguing doubts. If we live in the company of god, god is there to guide us in our actions. Learn to live with god to come up in life."

Speech of the religious speaker appealed to the student. He decided at once to live in the company of god and come up in life. By nature, he was devout. He dedicated further to praying to god. One year passed. The student did not experience any change for good in his life. He met the saintly man and said:

"In your speech a year ago, you said that living with god guides us on how to come up in life."

"I said rightly," said the saintly man.

"During the last one year, I have regularly offered prayers to god. But no change for good has come about in my life," said the student.

"But I said living with god helps," said the saintly man.

"Is offering regularly prayers to god not living with god?" said the student.

"No," said the saintly man.

"Then, what is living with god?" said the student.

"Understanding what greatness god stands for, what great things he has done and trying to do what the god has done," said the saintly man.

The student understood what living with god was, lived with god and became great in his life.

- - -

40. THE MUSICIAN

A musician in the court of a king was very famous for his musical works. He not only composed lyrics but also lent his voice to the lyrics. Everyone in the court immensely

liked performance of the musician. Hardly a day passed
without mellifluous performance of the musician in
private chamber of the king. The musician respected
the king and the king liked the musician the most. In
spite of closeness that made place between the king and
musician, the musician never abused his position. He
always remained very simple and unassuming.

Times do not remain the same forever. They keep
changing. The same happened in the case of the musician
too. The king that liked him the most suddenly got
withdrawn from him. He hardly invited the musician to
give his performance. Instead of listening to his music,
the king started listening to music of other artistes. The
musician felt hurt for sudden change in the king. He
said nothing. He bore the pain silently. When the king
did not give him a chance to perform for a long time, he
went to the chief minister and expressed his anguish. The
chief minister was erudite. He understood feelings of the
musician and said to him:

"If you want to gain back what you have lost, there is
something which you should do."

"What is it?" said the musician.

"Go to Kasi, have a holy dip in the Ganges, pray to
Lord Shiva and come back," said the chief minister.

"Will it help?" said the musician.

"Repose confidence in me," said the chief minister.

"It may take nearly year for me to make the journey,"
said the musician.

"Let it take. If you want the king to patronise you as
before, do as I say," said the chief minister.

The musician agreed to do what the chief minister said. He took permission of the king and set out on his long journey. He went to Kasi, did what he was ordained to do and returned home after one full year. The king heartily welcomed the musician, expressed his joy to see him after a long time and made him give a performance the same night. The musician gave his performance and pleased the king.

Next day, the musician met the chief minister, expressed that his trip to Kasi bore fruit and thanked him for his suggestion. The chief minister acknowledged thanks of the musician with a smile and said to himself:

"As long as you gave your performance regularly, the king could not make out how sweet was your music. He has come to know how sweet it is after tasting distasteful music from other musicians."

- - -

41. THE SOLITARY MONK

A warrior lost a war. He suffered a serious mental setback. He turned away from worldly life. He went on a tour in quest of peace. He went to the Himalayas. He saw a monastery on a hill slope. A monk ran it. The warrior liked tranquil ambience of the place. He went to the monk and said:

"I request you to permit me to stay here."

"This is a monastery. You may stay here," said the monk.

The warrior stayed with the monk for a few days. He observed that very few monks stayed in the monastery. One day, the warrior said to the monk:

"How old is this monastery?"

"It is very old," said the monk.

"There are hardly any monks here," said the warrior.

"No one comes to stay here," said the monk.

"Why?" said the warrior.

"Many people come here to join this monastery. But I dissuade them from doing that," said the monk.

"Why do you do so?" said the warrior.

"World is not a place of renunciation. It is a place for work. I want people to live in their place of work, not here," said the monk.

"Then why are you running the monastery?" said the warrior.

"To send people back to their place of work," said the monk.

The warrior was moved. He paid his respects to the monk and returned to his place of work. After a long time, he revisited the monastery to pay respects to the monk. There stood a king in place of the warrior.

- - -

42. DEVOTION

A man was a non-vegetarian. He liked non-vegetarian dishes. He hardly took food without non-vegetarian dishes. Every one jeered at him for his taste. But the man did not bother. He liked his taste and lived through his habit very happily, for a long time.

The man crossed his sixties. His mother passed away. He performed funeral rites of his mother in his home place, collected her ashes in a pot and went to Kasi to immerse the ashes in the holy river Ganges. A pundit at banks of the river performed rituals as per scriptures and said to the man:

"If you want salvation of your mother, you have to do something."

"What is it?" said the man.

"You have to give up what you like the most in your life," said the pundit.

"I am prepared to do it," said the man.

"What is it that you like the most?" said the pundit.

"Eating non-vegetarian dishes," said the man.

"Can you stop eating non-vegetarian dishes henceforth?" said the pundit.

"I can," said the man.

And the man stuck to his word. He stopped eating non-vegetarian dishes and never tasted the same for rest of his life.

- - -

43. STRENGTHS AND WEAKNESSES

A personnel officer worked for a company for a long time and became head of Human Resources Department by fag end of his service. On the final day of relinquishing his office, he called his successor to his cabin, handed over a secret file to him and said:

"This is a secret file. Keep it safely. It will help you a lot in discharging your duties."

"What does the file contain?" said the successor.

"It contains weaknesses of several employees working in this organisation," said the HRD head.

"How does it help me?" said the successor.

"You can exercise control over people by knowing their weaknesses," said the HRD head.

"I shall keep the file safely," said the successor.

The HRD head left the company. The successor took over HRD under his control. After one year, the new head met the former head in an informal get-together. The former head enquired:

"How are you?"

"I am fine," said the new HRD head.

"How is your company?" said the former HRD head.

"It is faring well," said the new HRD head.

"I hope you are using the file that I gave you," said the former HRD head.

"No," said the new HRD head.

"Why?" said the former HRD head.

"I built my own file," said the new HRD head.

"Where is the need for a new file?" said the former HRD head.

"There is," said the new HRD head.

"What is it?" said the former HRD head.

"You have acted on weaknesses of people. I am acting on strengths of people. The file what I built is of what strengths my people have got," said the new HRD head.

- - -

44. DEVOTION TO DEITY

A tribal man renounced worldly life and went to the Himalayas. He spent more than four decades in company of saints that dwelt in the mountains. He became old. He wanted to visit his place of birth before he breathed his last. He set out on foot towards his village that lay snugly tucked at foot of a hill inside thick forest. After many months, he reached his destination. He could not recognise his village. The forest that was there around the village was no more there. Deforestation took place in the place, in a big way. There were hardly any trees left out inside or in neighbourhood of the village.

The old man felt very sorry to see state of his village that looked bare like a shorn head. He pitied ignorance of the villagers that cut the trees. He advised his people to plant trees. But no one heeded his advice. He did not know what to do.

One day, right in the morning, priest of the village went hurriedly to see headman of the village and said to him:

"I had a strange dream yester night."

"What is it?" said the headman.

"The village deity appeared in my dream and said that she would take birth on top of the hill abutting our village on the ensuing full moon day," said the priest.

"It is great news. What else did the deity say?" said the headman.

"She told me the location on hilltop where she would appear and where a shrine is to be built for her. She also ordered that devotees must plant trees to cool the hillside, since the deity is red hot like a burning inferno," said the priest.

The headman believed the priest. He called all villagers and told them about dream of the priest. On the appointed day, all devotees went up to the hilltop to witness the divine miracle. What the priest dreamt came true. The deity of the village appeared in the form of a rock idol underneath a boulder. The villagers lifted up the idol with religious rituals and built a small shrine for the deity. They planted trees all over the hillside to show their devotion and respect for the deity.

The deity established herself on the hilltop, as a one possessing of many powers. Devotees from far and near thronged to the hill, to offer their prayers to the powerful deity. Invariably, whenever they went to the temple, they planted trees, as a mark of respect to the deity.

Within a few years, a mantle of green cover spread out on the hillside and the surroundings. The thick forest that existed there earlier returned to the place. The old man, who came from the holy mountains, went back with satisfaction. He did not forget to thank the priest that made things happen for him.

- - -

45. THE BLACK BIRD

A black bird lived in a deserted light house on the beach of a sea. The light house was abandoned long ago. None lived around the place. The black bird occupied the long rock built light house that overlooked the sea, enjoyed the rise and fall of the tides in sea and fed on the fish that abounded in sea waters of the place. It flew merrily all around during day time and rested for the night in a niche on top floor of the light house. It was blissfully happy. It was of the opinion that it lived in the most beautiful place on face of earth.

One morning, a green bird came from somewhere and descended on sea shore near the light house. It was very young. It looked very bright and shining under sunlight. It walked slowly on the wet sand. Apparently, it enjoyed scenic beauty of the place. The black bird greeted the green bird:

"Hello. I stay here in the nearby light house. Who are you? I never saw you in this part of the place previously. Where from have you come?"

"I belong to a different part of the land. Someone told me that this is a lovely location that one should see. I yearned to see this place for a long time. I am very happy because I came to see this place, at last," said the green bird.

The black bird was flattered. It felt very happy to hear appreciative words about the place that it lived in from a stranger. It said:

"How do you like it?"

"What I heard about this place is true. It is a lovely sightseeing place," said the green bird.

"This is the most beautiful spot in the world," said the black bird.

"There is no doubt. This is a very good beauty spot," said the green bird.

"There is no other beauty spot in the world that is as good as this," said the black bird.

"This is one of the best. There are some more beautiful spots in the world," said the green bird.

"How do you say so?" said the black bird, disapprovingly.

"Because I have seen some more beautiful places like this," said the green bird.

"I don't believe it. In my opinion, there is no beauty spot in the world that is better than this," said the black bird.

"Come with me. I shall show you," said the green bird.

The black bird did not like to hear that there existed some more beauty spots in the world. It wanted to prove the green bird wrong. It agreed instantly to the offer made by the green bird and flew with it on a journey to see other beauty spots.

The green bird took the black bird around the places that it had visited earlier. The itinerary that the birds followed was very long. It lay though many lands. The black bird was stunned to see many ravishing spots of beauty on its journey. It pitied the state of ignorance that it lived in, previously all along. It was full of admiration for the green bird. It said:

"I admit that you are right. I wonder how you have come to know about all these places and seen them."

"I roam around. I am a citizen of the world," said the green bird.

"I can understand. I am a denizen of my own dungeon," muttered the black bird.

- - -

46.   THE JESTER

There was a courtier in the service of a king. He was in charge of cultural activities to be organized in the fort. He took care of which shows were to be presented inside the fort, which artistes were to showcase their talent, schedule of the shows, honorarium to be paid to the artists and other aspects related to the job. He was very honest. He did his job meticulously well. He always ensured that he presented good shows that entertained royal guests inside the palace.

The courtier followed a custom. According to the custom, if any artist or group of artists wanted to give their shows inside the fort, they were to present the shows before him. The courtier gave chance to the aspiring performers to perform, only if he was impressed with the show given by them.

One day, a jester approached the courtier and requested him to give him a chance to showcase his performance inside the fort. The courtier heard that the jester gave public performances in many places and entertained audience. He did not object to request of the jester. He told the jester to give a maiden presentation before him and he could get a chance only if he was impressed by the show. The jester agreed. He gave a presentation before a select group of audience, in which the courtier also was present. The show was over. The courtier gave his opinion:

"I am sorry. I cannot give you a chance."

The jester was stunned. He did not expect that reply from the courtier. But he did not have cheek to question the courtier. He looked sadly into the face of the courtier and kept quiet. The courtier read feelings of the jester on his face and said:

"I know that my decision hurts you. But I feel you have not impressed me."

"Thank you, sir. You gave me an opportunity to present my show before you and make you laugh," said the jester.

The courtier suddenly realized that he laughed out loud all through the show and wondered why he said that he was not impressed. He took back his words and corrected himself. He gave the jester a chance to stage his performance before the royal guests.

- - -

47. TRANSFER OF KNOWLEDGE

A scholar in a shrine was a sad man. He was old. He was well versed in recital of Vedas. He wanted to transfer his knowledge on Vedas to his sons. But he could not do it, since none of his sons showed interest to learn it from him. He wanted to transfer the same to his grandsons. But he could not do it, since all his grandsons turned away from him with disinterest. Every day morning and evening, he sat in a remote corner of the shrine, and recited Vedas, all alone, mellifluously. Devotees, who visited the shrine, heard recital of the scholar with deep absorption. The scholar proffered to teach the Vedas to anyone, who showed interest to learn the same. But no one showed interest to learn from him.

More years added on the old man. It got seated in the mind of the scholar that he would have to die with knowledge in him not transferred to anyone. Many a time, he shed tears by thinking that the knowledge on Vedas what he received from his predecessors would die, once for all, after him. He prayed to god to give him a disciple to whom he could transfer his knowledge, before he was gone. The god was kind. The scholar's prayers were heard. One evening, when cows returned homewards and when lights in the shrine came on, a boy approached the scholar, offered his respectful obeisance and said to him:

"Sir, I have a request."

"Tell me," quivered tone of the scholar.

"May I request you to teach me recital of the Vedas," said the boy.

"That, I shall do gladly. But, tell me how keen are you to learn it from me," said the scholar.

"I am deeply interested to learn," said the boy.

"Remember that learning Vedas is not as easy as learning other subjects. It is to be done with deep devotion, discipline and dedication under the personal supervision of a master. If you vow to learn it with utmost commitment, I am prepared to teach you," said the scholar.

"I promise, I shall do it," said the boy.

"We shall start the learning session tomorrow," said the scholar.

"As you may be pleased," said the boy.

The scholar accepted the boy as his disciple and the boy accepted the scholar as his revered master. The transfer of knowledge started the next day, on a good note. The learning course continued for a few years, until the master felt that he transferred his knowledge to his disciple and the disciple developed confidence that he learnt what his master taught him. On last day of the learning course, the scholar was extremely happy. He asked his disciple to recite the Vedas that he learnt. The disciple recited. By the time the recital ended, the old scholar was no more. He breathed his last.

- - -

48. STATE OF MIND

There lived a father and his son in a town. Both were markedly different. The father wished from bottom of his heart that all people should be rich and no one should have necessity to ask for money. The son thought differently. He wished that all people should be in need of money. An angel, who observed behaviour of the two individuals for a long time, wanted to know from the son why he and his father behaved differently. One night, when the son was all alone on terrace of his house, she appeared before the son and said:

"I want to clarify a point."

"What is it?" said the son.

"There is a marked difference between you and your father on how you think about others," said the angel.

"You are right," said the son.

"May I know why such a difference is there between both of you," said the angel.

"My father is a miser and I am a money lender," said the son.

"How does it matter?" said the angel.

"My father is a miser. He does not want others to ask him for money. Therefore, he wants others to be rich. I am a money lender. I want people to be poor, such that they come to me for money," said the son.

The angel got shock of her life. She lifted herself up into air and flew away.

- - -

49. PUBLIC SERVANT

A king ruled a land that was a confluence of many ethnic cultures. He wanted overall development of all regions and development of the nation as a whole. He employed public servants belonging to a particular region in the same region by thinking that sons of soil worked better for development of their regions. But what happened was something different. The public servants did nothing to develop their regions. They used their local influence and consolidated themselves in their positions. They usurped funds released by the king for the purpose of regional development. The regions did not develop. On the other hand, the public servants developed. The malady did not end there. The public servants incited regional feelings and set people of one region against others. Regional spirit instead of national spirit took roots in minds of people.

The king noticed what happened. He sought advice from his courtiers on how to deal with the problem. He got a good suggestion from one of the courtiers. The suggestion given by the courtier was to post a public servant belonging to one region in any other region other than his own region. The king liked the suggestion and ordered for implementation of it. It met with tough resistance from his public servants initially. But things settled down soon to normalcy.

Posting of public servants in regions other than their own regions worked miracles. The public servants, who worked recklessly during their service in their own regions, worked responsibly, once they went out of their native lands. Since they no more wielded local support, they tried their best to prove their mettle and develop the regions in which they worked. The local public, impressed by the development, developed respect not only for the public servants, but also the regions from which the public servants hailed. In the long run, regional feelings paved way for fostering of national spirit among the public.

The king succeeded in accomplishment of what he desired. He richly rewarded the courtier that gave a game changing suggestion.

- - -

50.   REBELLION

The king of an island nation noted with concern that people in the island were very poor. He was a far sighted man. He wanted to develop the nation, create employment opportunities and raise living standards of his people. He worked out a plan. He constructed a sea port in a coastal front of the island and created all necessary facilities in the port for ships to halt and sailors and seafarers to stay. He invited sailors to make use of port facilities in the island.

The island was at a strategic location on a sea route that connected far flung coastal nations. The sailors found it convenient to take a break in their long journey and stay in the island for a brief period. They started using the port. Initially, very few ships, only from some nations, headed towards the port. But, over a period of time, ships, hailing from many nations from different directions, flocked to the island. Steadily, trading business increased manifold in the island and the island became a very important business hub. Many foreign nationals, who ran trading businesses, left their own nations, settled in the island, built houses and business centres and made the island their new homeland. Because of the business activities, the king got good revenue and locals got good employment opportunities. The king built a big port city adjacent to the sea port and created conditions congenial for residential and business operations in the place. The sea port and the port city buzzed and bustled with activity all throughout day and night, all through the year. The king was highly accommodative and impartial. He took care of people from outside the island as much as native inhabitants of the island. The island nation, under aegis of the visionary king, flourished and prospered.

A rebel, who was against the king, campaigned that due to myopia of the king, many lands of the island nation went into the hands of foreign nationals and unless the king was dethroned, justice would not be meted out to the native people. Many sons of soil believed the rebel and joined hands with him. In a coup, the king was overthrown. The rebel took over the throne. Some members of the rebellion attacked the non-locals, looted their properties and created panic in them. The non-locals, who made the island as their home nation, left the land and fled back to their native lands.

Uncanny peace returned to the island. No foreign ship ever came to halt there, thereafter. The island became purged of non-locals. Properties left behind by the non-locals went into hands of the locals. The local activists had a merry time. They succeeded to undo what the former king did. With loss of business and employment, the locals went back to do what their predecessors did for generations. Poverty, like darkness after nightfall, returned to the island, in a big way.

- - -

51. REMEMBRANCE

There lived a rich man and his wife in a town. The rich man loved his wife. But he was highly authoritative. He often spoke harshly to his wife. The wife was very mild and obedient. She never raised her voice against her husband. She discharged her duties dutifully and managed her house meticulously well.

The couple became old. Their children studied well and went away to foreign lands in search of lucrative jobs. The old couple, left to themselves in their house, lived together by themselves.

The old man did not leave his old habit. He shouted at his wife for every silly reason. But the wife did not say anything. As her husband lived with his old habit, she too lived with her old habit. She never reacted and spoke against her husband. She took things in a lighter vein with stoic silence.

More years passed. The wife fell sick. She was on her death bed. Doctors declared that she was in her last stage. The husband was shaken. He remained glued to bedside of his wife and served her. One day, the wife said to her husband:

"Very soon, I shall no more be there to take care of you. Take care of yourself."

The wife passed away. The husband perceived that a big vacuum made place in his life. He turned very sad. He built a beautiful memorial in the name of his wife and spent most of his time only in the temple. Often, when he was all alone, he rued:

"I should have been more kind to my wife, when she was alive."

- - -

52.   MENDICANT'S PREDICTION

A king had high concern for his subjects. He introduced many welfare schemes and created conditions conducive for comfortable living of his subjects. The subjects lived happily under rule of the king.

One day, a travelling mendicant happened to pass through the kingdom. He was highly impressed with how happily subjects of the kingdom lived and how the king cared for his subjects. He expressed his desire to see the king. Men of the king carried wish of the mendicant to the king. The king received the mendicant happily in his court hall in presence of other courtiers. The mendicant said:

"I came here to say a few good words about your rule."

"I shall be honoured to hear them," said the king.

"Your rule is excellent," said the mendicant.

"I am elated to hear it," said the king.

"There is no ruler in the entire neighbourhood that is as good as you," said the mendicant.

"It is exciting to hear it," said the king.

"But you are going to be in for a big problem shortly," said the mendicant.

"What is it?" said the king.

"Your kingdom will not long last," said the mendicant.

"Why do you say so?" said the king.

"People in your kingdom are not working," said the mendicant.

"Why they are not working?" said the king.

"Your rule is so good that there is no need for your people to work. The kingdom with people that do not work will become extinct very soon," said the mendicant.

The king took message from the mendicant and took corrective action in his rule. He created need for his people to work.

- - -

53. SWEETNESS OF LABOUR

A man, after studies, left his home town and went to a far off place for employment. Once in every one year, he made it a point to visit his home town, meet his childhood chums and visit places that he frequented in his childhood.

Every time when he paid a visit to his home town, invariably he visited a school that was situated in a slum. His friends did not understand why the man went to the school every time, whenever he visited his home town. One of his friends asked him:

"Why do you go to the school, whenever you come here?"

"I have some relation with the school," said the man.

"You have not studied there," said the friend.

"That is true," said the man.

"Then what takes you to the school?" said the friend.

"To see the school, in building of which, I lent my labour," said the man.

"What do you mean?" said the friend.

"When I was in my college, I joined a social service group. The group organised a labour camp in the school and as a part of it, I worked for one day in construction of the school building. That I lent my labour in construction of the school draws me to the school," said the man.

- - -

54.   WORK TO DO

There worked two young design engineers in a Company. Both were highly talented. But there was a marked difference in their mindsets. The first one accepted to do any type of job that was assigned to him. The second accepted a job, only if he liked it. As a result, the first one was always overloaded. He had sufficient work on hand at any given point of time. Whereas, the second one was relatively very free. He had jobs to do only occasionally.

Eventually the first one rose very fast in his career. He got fast track promotions, one after another and shot up to become chief executive of the Company. On the other hand, the second one got time scale promotions, now and then, reached middle management level and stagnated there. Thereafter, however hard he tried, he could not reach senior management level.

One day, in an interactive session arranged with new recruits of the Company, the chief executive delivered a welcome address and implored upon the youngsters to work hard to come up in life. After the address, one participant said:

"Sir, I want to know the secret of success in your career."

"Work," said the chief executive.

"Will you kindly elaborate on it," said the participant.

"Getting work to do is a great opportunity. Whenever it came to tap doors of my house, I readily opened doors and let it in. I never necessitated for it to turn away from me. It is the one that span success for me," said the chief executive.

- - -

55.   ONE AT A TIME

A writer had a problem. When he was leisurely, he had many ideas that flashed across in his mind. But when he sat down to work on the ideas, he failed to recollect them. However hard he tried, he could not call back to memory, what appeared in his mind earlier. He was very unhappy.

One day, the writer happened to go inside a forest, where he saw a hunter. The hunter with bow and arrows in his hands stood underneath a tree and targeted birds that flew freely in air. He appeared to be a very good marksman. He hardly missed his target. Every time he shot, invariably he brought down a bird.

The writer was highly impressed with marksmanship of the hunter. He went to the hunter and said:

"You are a very good marksman."

"That I am," said the hunter.

"When there are many birds in air, how are you able to see and shoot only one at a time?" said the writer.

"For you there are many birds in air," said the hunter.

"For you?" said the writer.

"Only one," said the hunter.

"What is it?" said the writer.

"The one that I want to shoot," said the hunter.

The writer got clue from what the hunter said. He changed his way of working. Instead of seeing through many ideas marching past in his mind and trying to remember them at a later time, he cultivated the habit of catching immediately an idea that flashed in his mind. Thereafter, he never let escape an idea that entered his mind space. He became a successful writer.

- - -

56. THE ROAMER

A young design engineer was very bright and brainy. He brought out excellent ideas in innovating new products as well as diagnosing functional problems of products. He was in good looks of top brass of his Company. But he had a problem. He rarely sat in his seat. Most of the times, he wandered around on roads inside the Company, sipped coffee in the canteen, moved about in garden watching plants, trees and birds and settling down to doing mundane and irrelevant jobs in his department.

Watch and ward that monitored movements of employees in the Company, noticed strange behaviour of the engineer for a long time and brought their observation to notice of chief executive of the Company. The chief executive called the engineer to his cabin and said:

"It is reported that, many a time, you are not found in your seat and loitering around on roads."

"Yes sir," said the engineer.

"Avoid it," said the chief executive.

"I cannot do it," said the engineer.

"Why?" said the chief executive.

"I can think only when I roam around and do nothing," said the engineer.

The chief executive blossomed into a smile and gave the young man free hand in what he did.

- - -

57.   PARTITION

Two brothers wanted to divide their ancestral property between them. The elder brother made two parts of the property with one part big and the other small and said to his younger brother:

"The two parts are before you. You may choose what you want."

"Why did you make one part big and the other small," said the younger brother.

"If you choose the bigger part, you will have our mother with you. If you choose the smaller part, you need not have mother with you," said the elder brother.

"If that is the case, I feel the partition is not properly balanced," said the younger brother.

"If you are not satisfied with my proposal, propose how we shall partition the property," said the elder brother.

"If you ask me, we should partition the property such a way that mother is on one side and our entire property is on other side," said the younger brother.

"And you want to choose the part that has our property," said the elder brother.

"No," said the younger brother.

"Then what will you choose?" said the elder brother.

"The part with mother," said the younger brother.

"Your proposal is acceptable to me," said the elder brother.

The two brothers reached an understanding in the presence of elders of the village and signed a deed. The elder brother pitied ignorance of his younger brother. The

younger brother pitied ignorance of his elder brother. After
the partition, the mother commented to her younger son:

"You have acted unwisely in your choice making."

"I have taken a very wise decision. You are worth more
than the property that my brother has taken," said the
younger son, pressing chin of his mother.

- - -

58. VALUE OF LABOUR

A young boy worked in a grocery shop run by a wholesaler.
After a few years of service in the shop, the boy realized
that work in the shop was more and he was getting
overworked. He left the job and joined a shop run by a
retailer. Work in the new shop was very less. But the boy
was not free. Even though there was no sufficient work
for the boy to do, the retailer created some or other job
and kept the boy busy all throughout the day. The boy
understood that the retailer gave him jobs, even though
the jobs were not useful to him, just because he employed
him in his service. The boy left the new job, went back to
his previous master and requested him to take him back
into service. The wholesaler said:

"I shall take you back into service, provided you
confide why you have left your new job."

"My new master is giving me jobs to do, even though
they are of no use to him," said the boy.

"You are paid to work. How does it matter what job
is given to you?" said the wholesaler.

"Human labour is very precious. It should be useful for either giver of work or doer of work or both. If it is not useful to any one, it is as good as abusing human labour. In my opinion, my labour is precious," said the boy.

The wholesaler took the boy back into service instantly.

- - -

59. AGITATION

Agitation by locals against non-locals was in full swing, in a city. Locals assembled in large groups in cross road junctions and shouted slogans against non-locals. They moved in processions and raised their voice against city administration. They ransacked and looted properties of non-locals and damaged public properties. They forced schools, cinema halls, business establishments and public transport systems to shut down their operations. They created terror in minds of non-locals that came from outside the city and settled in the city.

Police action to check agitators from taking law into their hands bore no fruit. Televised speeches by men in power appealing to public to maintain calm did not show improvement in the situation. Orders by law enforcers prohibiting movement of public in groups yielded no results. Agitators were on free run. No effort to check them worked. The agitation spread all throughout the city. But, height of it was in centre of the city, near an age old heritage structure.

One afternoon, agitators rallied from different directions of the city towards the heritage structure and culminated into a huge assemblage. A leader addressed the gathering for a long time, explained how the non-locals exploited resources of the city for their advantage and appealed to people there not to rest until the non-locals left the city. The public in the gathering hailed address of the leader that delivered a moving speech. After the meeting was over, the public dispersed and went away from the place in different directions. The leader, who addressed the gathering, was still in his place of address, with a handful of men around him. An old man, who resided in the locality, recognised the leader, met him and said:

"Do you remember me? I stay in the same locality, where you stay."

"Yes. I recognise you," said the leader.

"You have delivered a very good speech," said the old man.

"Thank you," said the leader.

"What is the agitation against? I could not follow it fully," said the old man.

"It is against non-locals that have come from other areas and settled in our city," said the leader.

"Is it so? If that is the case, you are agitating for a good cause," said the old man.

"I know you will appreciate," said the leader.

"But I wonder why you are agitating?" said the old man.

"Because, I am a local," said the leader.

"Yes. You are a local. I remember you very well. You came from somewhere and settled here forty years ago," said the old man.

Colours changed on face of the leader. The leader did not know how to react to the old man, in presence of other agitators around him. He said nothing. He could not face the old man. He slithered silently away from the place.

- - -

60. THE ATHEIST

A landlord had a big rice mill in the name of his wife. The rice mill, contained inside a big perimeter wall, had mills, drying floors, stock houses to stock paddy and rice separately, parking lot for bullock carts and other milling facilities and sale counters. It sprawled over a large track of land, situated in suburbs of a town, away from residential localities, and close to paddy fields. Many workers worked inside the mill premises. The mill worked, round the clock, during paddy season, and the place was always abuzz with human activity. Wife of the landlord managed the mill and the landlord visited the place, once in a while.

Wife of the landlord was a good manager. She spent most of her time only in the mill. She was kind and considerate. She never lost her temper on any one. She maintained very good human relations with workmen that worked in the mill and customers that visited the place. One and all respected the lady.

The landlord was an atheist. He did not believe in god. He never visited a temple in his life time. He was a member of an association of atheists. He campaigned against god. He vehemently opposed concept of god. His wife was an agnostic. She neither accepted god, nor opposed god. Work was worship and mill was temple for her.

Wife of the landlord died, all of a sudden. The workers that worked in the mill turned very sad. They mourned death of the lady. They opined that they would not come across a philanthropic lady like her. They discussed among themselves, collected donations and erected a small shrine in a corner of the mill compound. They offered prayers to the departed soul regularly. The landlord did not oppose the move. He joined hands with workers in the mill. He went to the shrine regularly to see idol of his wife in the form of a deity and offer prayers to her.

- - -

61. ONLY SON

A lady doctor, after retirement from active service, dedicated her life to social service. Once in every week, she visited an old age home situated in suburbs of the town, where she lived, along with some more ladies of her locality, with similar mindset. She took with her donations collected from philanthropists, gave them to the old age home and spent time talking to inmates of the home. Residents of the old age home looked eagerly forward to weekends, to talk to their week end guests that visited the home to spend time with them. The lady doctor not only spoke to residents of the home on their health related issues, but also enquired about their personal and family related issues. The empathetic tone of the doctor brought solace to the in house residents that led desolate lives in solitude.

Once, the lady doctor went on a long tour and returned only after one month. She hurried through her chores and went to the home to greet her old acquaintances there. He spoke to them, one by one, and came to know that an old couple joined the home recently and they stayed in a separate room. The doctor went to see the couple in their room. She greeted the couple, introduced herself and said to the old lady:

"When did you come here?"

"Around a month ago," said the old lady.

"Where are you from?" said the doctor.

"We are from a nearby place," said the old lady.

"How many children do you have?" said the doctor.

"We have two sons," said the old lady.

"Where are they?" said the doctor.

"They are in their own houses, not very far away from our house," said the old lady.

"If you are having two sons, why are you not staying with them?" said the doctor.

"Because we have two sons," said the old lady.

"What do you mean?" said the doctor.

"My sons are not able to decide with whom we should stay," said the old lady.

The lady doctor felt sorry for the old couple, but hid her feelings. She spoke to them for some time, gave them confidence and went away from there, on her rounds. She shuddered at plight of the old couple and irresponsibility of their sons. On way, she thanked her luck, because she had only one son.

- - -

62. HERITAGE STRUCTURES

A king toured his kingdom and noticed that there were many ancient structures in the kingdom, in highly rundown condition. Many of the archaeological structures of imposing beauty stood for artistic taste of his predecessor kings, who erected them in their times. The people, who created the master pieces, left the world long ago. But the structures, brought into being by the connoisseurs of art, remained to sing song of the bygone legendaries. The king noted that most of the structures were at the brink of extinction and they needed immediate repairs. He decided to save the heritage structures at any cost and released grants in large quantities for repair, maintenance and protection of the coveted structures. He put in place a project team to execute the job meticulously.

The team listed out heritage structures to be included in the project and prioritized the works. To start with, they selected for renovation an old temple, dating back to more than a thousand years ago, situated in a far flung village. The work on the temple started in a big way.

After one year, the king received news that renovation of the temple was completed and the temple was ready for inauguration by the king. He was happy. He grew curious to visit the site. Along with his royal paraphernalia, he moved with pomp to the site. He was stunned to see the work done at the site. The old temple was not in its place. A new temple stood in place of it. The king was pained. He was shaken. He said nothing. He returned at once to his palace and froze flow of funds from royal treasury, earmarked for preservation of heritage structures. He did not like to become a party for pulling down heritage structures at his own cost.

- - -

63.   THE CONQUEROR

The king of a kingdom was not satisfied with size of the kingdom that he ruled. He wanted to conquer the world and rule it as a supreme monarch. He decided to put his thought into action. He went to a saint and said to him:

"Be pleased to bless me. I want to conquer the world."

"Give up the idea. It is not good. You have a big kingdom. Rule it happily," said the saint.

"My kingdom is very small," said the king.

"Will you be happy, if you will conquer the world?" said the saint.

"I shall be," said the king.

"Go ahead. You will conquer the world. But mark my words," said the saint.

"What are they?" said the king.

"You will not be happy after you conquer the world," said the saint.

The king ignored last words of the saint, took leave of him and set out on a mission to conquer the world with a mighty army. He fought a series of wars and won them. He established his supremacy in every kingdom and unfurled his flag there. He conquered the whole world and became a monarch of monarchs. By the time he reached back his native state, he became pretty old. He wanted to rule the whole world from the throne that he sat on. But he found that many kingdoms that he invaded long ago ceded and separated out of his sovereignty. He wished to gain them back through war. But he could not do it, because of the age that weighed heavily on him. He settled down to rule the state that he possessed in the start. He felt in heart of hearts that he should have heeded advice of the saint that forbade him from the misadventure.

- - -

64. HONESTY

An old lady served as a domestic help in the house of a rich man. The rich man's wife was very kind. She not only paid monthly salary to the maid, but also provided free food to the help. The help took part of her salary and saved the rest with the rich man's wife. One day, out of curiosity, the rich man's wife asked the help:

"What will you do with the money that you are saving with me?"

"To meet funeral expenses after my death," said the old lady.

"Why do you say so? You have your son to look after you," said the mistress.

"After I am gone, I do not want to become a burden to anyone," said the old lady.

Many years passed. During the time, the rich man lost his property and became poor. The old lady continued to be in service in his house.

One morning, the domestic help did not turn up for work. The rich man and his wife wondered why the help did not come for work, because she never absented. After a while, son of the old lady came and informed that his mother passed away, all of a sudden. The rich man and his wife were shaken. They felt very sad. The rich man's wife rushed inside her room, opened a closed box, took out of it a cloth sack of money, gave it to son of the old lady and said:

"Take this money and spend for funeral of your mother."

Son of the old lady went away and finished funeral of his mother. After the funeral was over, the rich man said to his wife:

"It appears you gave lot of money to the help's son."

"Yes," said the rich man's wife.

"Why?" said the rich man.

"It is not my money. It is the maid's money. The old lady saved money with me for a long time," said the rich man's wife.

"Does anyone know that the old lady saved money with you?" said the rich man.

"No," said the rich man's wife.

"What could have happened had you not revealed it to son of the old lady?" said the rich man.

"I can't even think of it," said the rich man's wife.

"Why?" said the rich man.

"The poor lady believed me. I can't cheat her," said the rich man's wife.

- - -

65. FINISHING TOUCH

A litterateur was a worried man. He wrote many works. But the works did not see light of the day. All of them lay piled up in a shelf and collected dust. The man often expressed to his friends that he was an unfortunate man and works created by him never saw light of the day.

The litterateur had a friend, who had contacts with a publishing house. The friend contacted editor of the publishing house, told him about his litterateur friend and arranged for a meeting between the litterateur and editor of the publishing house. The editor received the litterateur warmly and said to him:

"What did you write?"

"I penned quite a few works. The works include essays, stories, plays, musings and travelogues," said the litterateur.

"That is very nice to hear about. Did you not try to bring them out in print?" said the editor.

"I have not tried so far," said the litterateur shyly.

"In case you want to publish with us, you may submit your works for our consideration," said the editor.

"I shall be delighted to do so," said the litterateur.

"When can you submit?" said the editor.

"In a day," said the litterateur confidently.

"Well, I shall wait for you tomorrow. Please come and meet me with your works," said the editor.

"Sure. I shall do it. Thank you for your courtesy," said the litterateur, surfeited with joy.

The litterateur left office of the editor and went home. He stood before his works and tried to pick up for submission the best from them. He picked up a one, scanned through it, put it aside, picked up another, scanned through it, put it aside and did the same with several works that were before him. He could not decide which work to submit, because none of the works was fully finished. His promise to see the editor with his work, the next day, did not come through.

- - -

66. BENCHMARKING

The head of BCD Company selected benchmarking as a way to improve working standards in the Company. He called for a high level meeting of all group heads in the Company and spoke to them on the importance of benchmarking. He gave illustrated examples of how various companies in the world adopted benchmarking and how they achieved unimaginable improvement in their outputs. He impressed upon his group heads that benchmarking was need of the hour and all of them individually and collectively ought to try for implementation of the path breaking concept. All group heads in the meeting agreed unanimously to adopt benchmarking. After a prolonged deliberation, the head of the Company, in consultation with his senior colleagues, constituted a three member committee, tasked with the responsibility of implementing benchmarking. The meeting ended.

Members of the benchmarking committee met a number of times, deliberated on their task, took opinions of group heads in the Company and brought out a comprehensive report. They put in the report, which were the best performing industrial units in the city, which of them could be benchmarked and what benchmarks they should set for themselves. They submitted their report to head of the Company.

The head went through report of the committee and found that CDE Company was one of the best performing industrial units in the city. He decided at once that the Company was to be benchmarked. He made a list of officers to visit CDE Company and wrote a letter to head of CDE Company indicating that a team of officers from his Company wanted to visit CDE Company to study way of working there for the purpose of benchmarking and requested permission for the visit.

Incidentally, the same day, the head of BCD Company received a letter from head of CDE Company indicating that a team of employees from his Company wanted to visit BCD Company to study way of working there for the purpose of benchmarking and requested permission for the visit.

- - -

67.   APPROVER

A gang of bandits committed a series of thefts in a land ruled by a king. The bandits were very clever. They committed thefts in different parts of kingdom, in most unexpected times, and created panic among the subjects. The king spread a network of intelligence sleuths all over the kingdom, to get clues about whereabouts of the bandits. He sent armed corps in search of all suspected hideouts of the bandits. But the bandits escaped intelligence network spread by the king. They continued with their unlawful activities. The king and his establishment were deeply worried.

The king was helpless. He understood that he and his forces could do nothing to nab the culprits. He thought differently and decided upon a plan. He ordered for a public announcement. The announcement said that if the bandits surrendered they would be let off with minor punishment. Even the announcement did not work for some time. Ultimately, it paid dividend. One day, a member of the gang of bandits surrendered to the royal forces. Other bandits were still at large. They did not turn up to surrender. The royal corps prevailed upon the bandit, who surrendered, and elicited from him details of who was the gang leader, where the gang stayed, how the gangsters operated and where the plunder was hidden. Based upon the details, the corps swooped upon other members of the gang and punished them as per law of the land. The jury that tried the case said to the king:

"What shall we do with the gangster that surrendered to us?"

"Award him with means for livelihood," said the king.

"But, he has committed many crimes," said the jury.

"He has turned approver. I cannot punish an approver. If I do it, none in future will ever turn approver," said the king.

The jury agreed with the king and created means of livelihood for the bandit.

- - -

68. HELL AND HEAVEN

An employee in a factory was highly dissatisfied. He did not like factory way of working. He felt that coming to office early in the morning, slogging for nine hours in the factory and reaching back home in evening, fully tired, were nothing short of drudgery. He developed distaste for everything that he did inside the factory. Initially he kept his feelings about the factory to himself. But, over a period of time, he started sharing his feelings openly with others.

One afternoon, when it was time for lunch break, he got up from work, went to wash room, washed his hands and proceeded towards main gate of the factory. Still there were two minutes before the siren was to blow and main gates were to open. The employee felt restless to wait for two minutes. He vented out his feelings to a co-employee, who stood beside:

"What a factory we are working in. The management is so strict that they are not allowing us out of gate even two minutes before our lunch time."

"Yes. The present management is highly rule driven," said the co-employee.

"This is really a hell for us to work," said the employee.

General Manager of the factory happened to be nearby. He heard what the employee said, approached him and said to him:

"What you said is right. For insiders, inside is hell and outside is paradise. But for outsiders, inside is paradise and outside is hell."

The employee was shocked. He never expected that the General Manager could be around there. He could not face the General Manager. He lowered his head in shame for the words that he spoke.

- - -

69. CRITICISM

There lived a group of saints in a devotional centre, situated atop a hill in a forest. The saints spent their times in various spiritual activities in the centre, all throughout the year, excepting for two months. Once in every six months, they went in different directions to villages near and far and preached to worldly people, god related matters. With every saint, a novice, who joined the centre to become a saint, accompanied to know about what a saint in his life could do and how to interact with commoners. The devotional centre, established many generations ago, earned good name among public. Whenever the saints went out to see people, the people received them very warmly and receptively.

Once, a saint accompanied by his young disciple, went on a tour to visit some villages far away from the devotional centre. During their trip, they interacted with many villagers, took part in religious activities organized in temples and other public places, delivered talks and started back on their return journey. One afternoon, after they travelled on foot for a long distance, they were tired. They took rest under a wayside tree. The disciple said to the saint:

"Sir, I would like to ask a question."

"Ask," said the saint.

"You are doing selfless service to public in the name of god. But some people are passing hurting comments about you," said the disciple.

"What are they commenting about?" said the saint.

"They are commenting that we are worthless, wandering around doing nothing," said the disciple.

"If we are worthless, let us accept their comments," said the saint.

"But we are not worthless," said the disciple.

"If we are not worthless, let us ignore their comments," said the saint.

The disciple understood that he really was with a great saint. He learnt a lot from association of the saint and became a great saint, in course of time.

- - -

70.   KING IN PLACE

A lion was king of a forest. A talk started in the forest that the king was very passive. The talk slowly gained momentum and snowballed into a revolt against the king. Under pressure of the revolt, the king stepped down. With him, the royal establishment broke down. Inhabitants of the forest felt very happy to remove a king that was not active in his role. They felt that there was no need of a king and therefore position of the king remained vacant. The forest went without a king.

With no king in place, it was a free time for everyone in the forest. Everyone moved in the forest as he liked. Common code of discipline that remained in place hitherto gave place to indiscipline. The wild predators preyed freely on the tame creatures. The weak and meek feared to come out of their hideouts for fear of the ferocious hunters. Anarchy set in the forest. The fittest survived and the weakest perished.

Some noble souls in the animals felt that what happened in the forest after removal of the king was not good for anyone in the long run. They convened a meeting of all dwellers in the forest and impressed upon them the need to put a king in place immediately. Majority agreed. All of them went to the dethroned lion and requested him to take back reins of the animal kingdom. The lion agreed and put in place a royal establishment to help support him in his rule.

The king ruled as passively as before. But there was a sea change in attitude of the animals. They stuck meticulously to a common code of conduct that was in place previously and behaved responsibly. The king in place worked wonders.

- - -

71.   THE THIEF

A thief heard that a saint, who lived with a disciple in his thatched hut in suburbs of a village, had a precious treasure in his house. He desired to steal the treasure. He collected information that the treasure was inside a metallic chest in a corner of the house. One dark night, when the saint and his disciple were fast asleep, he sneaked into the hut, located the chest, took it into his hands and escaped out of the place safely.

In the morning, the disciple, while sweeping floor with a broomstick, noticed that the chest was not in its place and informed the same to the saint. The saint understood that the chest was stolen. But he was not perturbed. He said to his disciple:

"Don't worry. Nothing will happen to the chest. Either it will come back to us within a day or after one year."

"How do you say so?" said the disciple.

"I am confident," said the saint.

The saint and his disciple waited for one day. The chest did not come back. But exactly after one year, a learned man came with the stolen chest in his hands, returned the chest, fell prostrate on floor at feet of the saint, got up, stood with folded hands and said:

"Thank you. I am changed."

The saint blessed the man. The man took leave and went away. The disciple who witnessed the strange scene did not understand what passed before his eyes. He said to the saint:

"Who is this man?"

"The thief that stole the chest one year ago," said the saint.

"Why did he return the chest that has invaluable treasure in it," said the disciple.

"There are two caution notes in it," said the saint.

"What is written on the first caution note?" said the disciple.

"Return the chest in a day, if you don't want the treasure in this. If you don't do it, you will die in two days," said the saint.

"What is written on the second caution note?" said the disciple.

"Read the palm leaves in this chest, if you want to know where a big treasure trove is hidden," said the saint.

"How did the caution-notes help?" said the disciple.

"The first caution note gave option to the thief to return the chest, if he did not find it useful. The second one made the thief read to know where the treasure lay," said the saint.

"Did he get to know where the treasure is?" said the disciple.

"The thief returned the chest, only because he came to know where the treasure is," said the saint.

"Where is the treasure?" said the disciple.

"Within him," said the saint.

- - -

72. TALKING TREES

A boy broke rocks on a hillside, along with his father. He sweated under hot son. He wanted to take rest for a while. He found no shade anywhere nearby. He spotted two trees at base of the hill. He went down the hill and relaxed under the trees. He felt as if he was in the lap of his mother. When he was about to slip into sleep, he heard the trees talking to each other. He lent his ears to the talk. There was a conversation on between the mother tree and child tree.

"Mother," said the child.

"Tell me my child," said the mother.

"Don't you think that we are the most unfortunate souls on this earth?" said the child.

"Why do you say so?" said the mother.

"We are all alone here," said the child.

"Yes," said the mother.

"Don't we have our kith and kin?" said the child.

"We had them, once upon a time," said the mother.

"Now," said the child.

"We don't have anyone," said the mother.

"What happened to them?" said the child.

"All of them perished," said the mother.

"How?" said the child.

"They are felled," said the mother.

"How many were there earlier?" said the child.

"Many. We had a plant kingdom of our own. With countless trees spread all over the earth, we ruled the world, at one point of time," said the mother.

"Why were the trees felled? What harm did we do for others?" said the child.

"We have not caused any harm to anyone. Instead, we have done many things good to others," said the mother.

"Who has made us bereaved?" said the child.

"The man," said the mother.

"Can no one save us?" said the child.

"God only can save us," said the mother.

"Why we should not pray to god to come to our rescue?" said the child.

"That I am doing," said the mother.

"When will he come to save us?" said the child.

"When he feels that our existence on earth is required," said the mother.

"From today onwards, I too shall pray to god to come and save us," said the child.

"Do it," said the mother.

The boy under the trees was moved with the conversation that took place between the trees. He took pity for sad plight of the trees. He got up and looked at the trees. He made up his mind to do something for the trees. He walked away from the place.

From next day onwards, whenever the boy got break from his work, he planted trees and watered them on the hillside. The child tree saw the boy with wonder and said to her mother:

"I am very happy. The boy is planting trees all over the place."

"The god has come to save us," said the mother tree.

- - -

73.   FIRST IN COMMAND

The elected head of a nation faced many corruption charges and enquiries. He braved opposition, until it was only from other political parties. When the opposition started in his own party, he could no more stand it.

Under pressure from his party men, against his will, with great difficulty, he stepped down at last, to give room for another person to take over his position. Since, incidentally, he happened to be head of the political party that was in power, he called for emergency meeting of his party executive committee and named a person who was very obedient to him to become his successor.

The new head took charge from his predecessor. The former head thought that his trusted lieutenant was in power and he could continue to have his say in governance of the nation. But the new head acted differently. He became a hard nut to crack. He ignored instructions of his mentor and acted independently. He took decisions that were good for public and his party. He did nothing to please his earlier boss. With path breaking changes in administration, he proved himself to be one of the best heads.

One day, wife of the new head said to him:

"I have a doubt."

"Tell me," said the new head.

"Earlier, when you handled a ministry under the old head, you got the name that you never took any decision on any issue. Now, you are a completely changed man. The way you are handling your portfolio is exemplary. Can you say how such a big change came over you within no time?" said wife of the head.

"Earlier, I was second in command. Now I am first in command," said the new head.

- - -

74. IT MATTERS WHO MANS

The state of affairs of a Government run public hospital was highly deplorable. Patients that visited the hospital tasted hell on earth. Many complaints went to the Government against the hospital administration. But no remedial action was initiated.

Ultimately media entered the scene with a big bang. When a series of reports against the hospital appeared in papers and were telecast in channels, the Government swung into action. They removed administrator of the hospital and put a new one in place of him. The new administrator took charge of the hospital, but did pretty nothing to change scenario in the hospital. He remained as callous as the old one. When he did nothing for nearly two months, the staff in the hospital took it for granted that the new one was no way different from the old one and they continued their old practices unchecked. The new head waited calmly until he felt that it was time for him to act and he acted firmly. He called various associations of employees in the hospital, one by one, and told them to work dutifully. He let off those that fell into line and complied with his instructions. He cracked whip on those that revolted against him. People that got used to easy earnings could not tolerate deep dip in their earnings. They staged sit-ins and sit-outs, shouted slogans and wore black badges, showing their resentment to dictatorial attitude of the new administrator. But none of them cut ice with the new head. People could not continue to fight for long against the establishment. They gave up their struggle. They changed themselves. Services in the hospital improved. Patients were highly pleased with marked change of affairs in the hospital. Media appreciated the new head. Government congratulated him for his commendable work.

The administrator worked very hard, round the clock to improve facilities in the hospital. Every day, he made visits to wards and made surprise checks. Every day, he met association heads and inspired them to do better. Staff members of the hospital, who were initially dead against the head, turned into his fans, over a period of time. The greatest quality, which marked style of working of the new head, was he never took any punitive action against anyone working in the hospital. The hospital, with improved medical facilities and increased patient turnout established for itself very good name, very soon. The dirty name that it carried earlier was erased completely.

After his fixed tenure of stay was over, the administrator went on transfer to a different hospital. A new man took over his place. The staff that worked in the hospital earlier continued to work there. But absence of the change maker administrator had its effect. The hospital fell back into its old style of working.

- - -

75. RETURN TO MOTHERLAND

A professional after studies in his hometown, migrated to a foreign land and spent fifty long years of his life there. After retirement from service, he bought a house in capital city of the foreign land and settled there. After he spent a few months of retired life, he got disenchanted with monotonous and uneventful stay in the city. He remembered frequently days, incidents, friends and places of his native place. He particularly remembered his ancestral house that his forefathers constructed, school, which happened to be a building with archaic architecture, built by erstwhile rulers, a river full of water that skirted outskirts of the town, ancient temples with imposing rock structures dedicated to various gods and goddesses, lush green paddy and sugarcane fields, parks with ponds and walkways, conference halls, where lectures by eminent speakers were organised every week, public places, where political meetings took place occasionally, public and private libraries, where long rows of racks with books enticed readers, thickly crowded market places with a maze of narrow roads, incidents that made deep impact on him and acquaintances that he had association with. He lived physically in the foreign land. But mentally he lived in his hometown. Over a period of time, he developed a strong desire to leave the place where he lived, go back to his home town and settle there permanently for rest of his life.

No sooner did the thought of going back to his homeland enter his mind, he made it known to his family members, hurried through preparing for his return and landed back in his home town, after over fifty long years. The prospect of seeing physically what he saw in his virtual world for a long time filled him with euphoria. He did not walk on feet. He floated in air. He put up in a hotel and went out to see what all he saw before he left the place, half of a century ago.

He disbelieved his eyes. He saw nothing in the town that he was acquainted with. He tried to go to various places that he moved about in his childhood. But he could not do it. No place that he knew about was in its place. Geography of the entire town was changed beyond recognition. He felt as if the old town was totally razed to ground and a new town with completely new configuration came up in its place. After wandering aimlessly through the town for a whole day, he felt that he was not in his home town, but a foreign land. He was disappointed.

He returned to hotel in the evening, upset fully. He made up his mind not to stay in the foreign land that he was not acquainted with and return to the foreign land that he was acquainted with. He packed up his belongings that he did not even unpack fully and left for the foreign land that he came from.

- - -

76. MEDIATION

A small argument that started between a young wife and her husband led to a major scuffle between them. The wife left her home, went to her parents and started living separately. Husband was in his house, all alone. After a few days, the wedded partners revealed to their parents about why they lived separately. Parents mediated to resolve the differences that cropped up between the two youngsters. But they failed in their attempt. Over passing of time, they took sides of their own children and started blaming each other. Even intervention of community heads did not yield any results.

With passing of time, things did not change. In fact, they worsened. Elders of both the sides decided to move a court for divorce. The young couple were perturbed to know that their parents moved towards getting a divorce for them. But they were helpless. They could do nothing. They did not have cheek to challenge decision of their parents. They simply remained passive, looking silently at what the elders did.

The case of divorce went into the hands of lawyers. The lawyers used all their brilliance to establish that there was real need for a divorce. In the process of it, they fabricated charges that maligned characters of the married couple. The case went on for years. Hearings after hearings took place in court. Both sides waited expectantly for a final outcome. But the hearings never concluded for a final verdict to come out.

One day, the separated wife and husband happened to meet in a temple. They were touched to see each other after many years. The wife said:

"It is there in a court notice that my character is bad. Is my character bad?"

"No," said the husband.

"Why is such a charge made against me?" said the wife with a choked voice.

"I have not framed any charge against you," said the husband.

"I am told that many bad things are told against you in court. But I have not uttered anything that maligns your image," said the wife.

"I know it," said the husband.

"Do we want a divorce?" said the wife.

"No," said the husband.

"Why are we fighting the case in court?" said the wife.

"We are not fighting it. Our elders are fighting it," said the husband.

"What mistake did we do that has complicated our case and made it beyond our control?" said the wife.

"We have allowed mediators to handle our case," said the husband.

"Can we not reunite?" said the wife.

"That we shall do right now," said the husband.

"What shall we do with the case in court?" said the wife.

"Let our elders handle it," said the husband.

The separated wife and husband joined hands, took blessings of god in the temple and went back home to live together.

- - -

77. RIGHTEOUS LIFE

A young scholar wanted to lead a righteous life. He studied scriptures to know what the righteous life was. He interacted with many saints to know about what he wanted. He went to religious discourses to get clarity on the subject. But he did not get the clarity. Everyone, whom the scholar contacted, was very clear about what righteous life was. But there was no unanimity among views expressed by various people. Everyone gave his own definition. The scholar was confused. He did not know how to lead a righteous life.

One evening, the scholar sat thoughtfully on steps leading down to a river and looked at flowing waters of the river. A priest that took bath in the river, down below, came climbing up the steps to him and said:

"What makes you low in spirits, young man?"

"I want to lead a righteous life. But I am not able to decide what exactly righteous life is," said the scholar.

"If that is what is worrying you, I can clarify your doubt," said the priest.

"I shall be relieved, if you do it," said the scholar.

"Lead life that is right in your view. That is the most righteous life that you can lead in the world," said the priest.

"How do you say so? There are many divergent views on this, even in religious texts," said the scholar.

"There are divergent views in religious texts, because the texts cover righteous lives led by many great men and each great man has led a righteous life, in his own way," said the priest.

The scholar got answer for his intriguing doubt. He got up to live a life that he considered righteous in his own view.

- - -

78. LEGACY

A money lender was in twilight of his life. He worked hard, amassed wealth and led a happy life, with his children and grand children living with him in his family. Materialistically, he was quite well off. But, in bottom of his heart, he felt that he led a mediocre life and he achieved nothing very significant that he could look back and feel proud of. The thought that he could not do anything great in his life pricked him. He turned very pensive.

One day, he went to a religious congregation, where a speaker elaborated upon purpose of life. After the discourse was over, the man went to the speaker and expressed his problem. He said:

"You must help me find a solution for a problem that is troubling me."

"Tell me your problem," said the speaker.

"Of late, I am feeling that I have not done anything great in my life and that is paining me," said the money lender.

"This happens with everyone, who lives a life with no purpose," said the speaker.

"I am close to end of my life. I have not done anything worthwhile so far in my life. I am afraid to think that I shall not be able to face my death, if I am to die soon," said the money lender.

"You are right. Great is the man who dies with satisfaction that he has done something great in his life. A man who has not done anything great will have to breathe his last with a feeling that he has not done anything great," said the speaker.

"Will you please extricate me from this excruciating pain?" said the money lender.

"I can help you, if you want," said the speaker.

"Please suggest to me what great work I can do," said the money lender.

"What you do is not very important. You may do anything that you feel the best. But do such a work that leaves behind you your legacy. It is the one that gives you satisfaction and will long last, after you are gone," said the speaker.

The money lender thought of what he should do. He was not educated. He did not know how to do a great work. He thought and thought about what to do and struck upon a novel idea. He spoke to wealthy people in his town, solicited their cooperation and participation and started a private cooperative bank with a lion share in it in his name. Very soon, the bank started its operations and met needs of customers at reasonable money lending rates.

The money lender died. But the bank started by him continued after him. People of the town, in appreciation of pioneering services rendered by the money lender, changed name of the bank and named it after the money lender.

- - -

79. INCORRIGIBLE CHARACTER

There worked a boss and assistant in a factory. Both were highly qualified mechanical engineers. Boss was a prime mover, go getter and task master, always obsessed with work. Assistant was a man of different stuff. He was a work avoider, layabout and slacker, always shirking away from responsibilities. The boss was highly unhappy with his assistant. He tried hard to bring change for good in his assistant. But the assistant never felt the need for change and he never changed. Very often, the boss lost his temper and came down upon his assistant for his thoughtless works. Highlight of the situation was the boss shouted at and the assistant never reacted. The non-reaction from the assistant only added to fuel further, anger of the boss. Days passed with fireworks becoming common between the boss and assistant and both officers lived together with deep mutual mistrust and disrespect.

One morning, boss called the assistant, asked him to associate with tryout of a newly made tool and confirm that the component made out of the tool was acceptable. The assistant carried out instruction of his boss and reported back to him that the component made out of the tool was acceptable.

Go ahead clearance was given for mass production of the component from the newly made tool and, in the final assembly, the component was rejected for dimensional defects. Head of the factory called the boss and bombarded him. The boss could not face the head. He lowered his head in shame, returned to his cabin, called his assistant and said:

"Gentleman, you made a mess of things. You don't know how to do a job. Because of your foolish act, I had to eat a humble pie before my boss."

"What happened, sir?" said the assistant.

"Components made out of the tool cleared for production by you are found to be defective," said the boss.

"Mistakes happen sometimes, sir," said the assistant.

"Gentleman, I don't know what to say. I am really fed up with you. For god's sake, learn from me how to do a job, at least before I die," said the boss.

"Sorry sir. You will not die," said the assistant.

- - -

80. DARING POET

A great king wanted translation of Maha Bharatha in Telugu. He requested his court poet to take up the task and contribute to enrich literature of the vernacular language. The poet started the monumental work. But he could not finish it. He completed two and half chapters from the original work in Sanskrit and attained heavenly bliss. Thereafter, for nearly two centuries, no poet dared take up the unfinished work for completion. At last, another great poet took up the unfinished work of translation starting from third chapter and finished fifteen long chapters right up to the end. He did not attempt completing third chapter that his predecessor left unfinished. Since second half of the third chapter was not translated, the translation work as a whole remained unfinished for another hundred years. At last, another great poet took up translation of the unfinished third chapter to complete translation of a monumental work as a whole.

When the third poet attempted translating the unfinished third chapter, his well wishers cautioned him:

"Don't take up the work."

"Why?" said the third poet.

"Translating third chapter is inauspicious. That is why the first poet passed away before completing it," said his well wishers.

"I have decided to take up translation of unfinished part of the third chapter. I don't regret, if I die before I finish it. But if I live and finish it, I shall get the credit of handing over fully translated epic to my people," said the poet.

The poet hesitated no more. He took up translating a small part that left a great work unfinished. He finished it successfully. What he did in comparison to other two poets was very marginal. But he got the credit of finishing an epic that took nearly three centuries for translation from Sanskrit and got his place in trinity of poets that translated the monumental work.

- - -

81. GRAMMAR

A farmer turned poet composed devotional verses based on rules of prosody. Every word that he composed was pregnant with thought. Every line that he composed was metrical, musical, mesmerising and moving. The poet, with his enchanting works, won hearts of people. He created sensation in literary circles. He impressed public that turned into his fans.

Critics reviewed works of the poet, tested them on touchstone of grammar and concluded that there were many grammatical mistakes in the works and the works could not be treated as standard works from linguistic point of view. They commented that unlettered men attempted literary works, which only men of letters could attempt. The comments hardly hit the poet, because the poet remained away from literary associations, blissfully happy in his own world of creation and confined to his farming. The poet continued to write the way that he wrote hitherto with great passion and his works met with instant success in public.

The poet passed away. A few generations passed after death of the poet. But works of the poet continued to linger in the minds of many people. They, over generations, attained immortality.

After a few generations, some reviewers took up works of the bygone poet for a critical study and found in them many new usages that did not fit into grammar. They did not know how to correlate the usages with grammatical rules that ruled the language until then. They discussed, deliberated, discoursed and finally came to terms with usages introduced by the verse writer. They modified rules of grammar such that they accepted usages of the poet.

- - -

82. WHAT TO DO

A man worked very hard. He sincerely wished to come up in life and achieve something very big. But however hard he tried, he remained where he was and he did not rise in life. He was exasperated. He turned sad. He tried to introspect where he went wrong and how to correct himself. But he found no solution. He decided to take help from a consultant and contacted him.

The analyst heard problem of the man patiently and put to him a series questions. He asked what the man wanted to achieve, what he did towards accomplishment of his goal, what works he worked on, what works he finished, what works were there yet to be finished, his daily routine and many more questions pertinent for the analysis. Ultimately, after the interaction, the analyst got information that he wanted to get from his client, analysed the data, found out a solution and said to the client:

"I found out the reason why you are not able to progress in your life."

"What is it?" said the client curiously.

"You are not doing what you are supposed to do. You are doing what is not required to be done," said the analyst.

The client agreed with finding of the analyst. He thanked the analyst for his revelation, corrected his nature that prompted him to do what he liked rather than what was required and achieved what he wanted to achieve in his life, very soon.

- - -

83.   THE GOOD AUNT

A boy hailed from a poor family in a village. He went to his aunt's house in a nearby town, studied there from school to college and finished his graduation. Thereafter, he got a good job in government service in state capital, left the town, settled down in the capital, got promotions in quick succession, rose very fast in his career and became a very big bureaucrat.

After many years, the bureaucrat went on official visit to the town, where he studied. Officers of lower rung in the town made elaborate arrangements to receive the bureaucrat in a big way, put him up in best of the accommodation available in the town and take care of him during his stay in the town. The bureaucrat stayed along with his family members in a state guest house, specially spruced up for his visit. The officers put in charge of the visit chalked out a plan of which places the bureaucrat was to visit, whom to meet in the town and what to do during his stay in the place. They included in the itinerary the lower middle class locality where the bureaucrat stayed with his aunt in his earlier days. The bureaucrat saw the list of places that he was to visit officially and felt embarrassed to visit the place where house of his aunt was located. He did not revisit house of his aunt, after he left the town long ago. He found it very delicate to make it known that he was nephew of a lady that stayed in the locality. But he kept his feelings to himself. He did not reveal them to anyone.

On the appointed day, he went on a visit to various places in the town and, as a part of it, went to the locality, where he spent his long transformative years, many years ago. People of the locality gathered in good numbers to greet the guest that visited their locality. The bureaucrat saw for his aunt in the crowd. The lady was not there to be seen. After he left the crowd, he went to the house where her aunt stayed. The house was locked. He enquired about her with a neighbour. The neighbour said:

"She is not at home. She went on a pilgrimage trip."

"When did she go?" said the bureaucrat.

"Today morning," said the neighbour.

The bureaucrat understood that her aunt went away purposefully from the place in order not to cause embarrassment to him.

- - -

84. HUNGER FOR LOVE

A householder felt that his aged parents, who lived with him in his house, became a big burden for him. He could not decide how to get rid of them. He wanted to put them up in an old age home. But, afraid of criticism by others, he refrained from doing it. He pulled on with his parents for some more time, until he felt that he could no more have them in his house. He firmed up his mind. He took a hardened stand. He informed his parents that he wanted to admit them in an old age home. Much against interest of the parents, he took them to an old age home and admitted them in it.

The old age home was a paid home. It was well managed. The home treated inmates of the house kindly and warmly. Attendants in the home attended to various needs of the inmates. Doctors checked them up regularly. Social workers from service organisations and personnel from media visited the home regularly and interacted with the aged persons to know about how they were faring. Management of the home organised prayers, religious discourses, and entertainment programmes daily to engage the aged.

The householder went, once in a while, to see his parents in the home. The parents expressed that they were very comfortable in the home and told their son not to take pain of visiting them again and again. The householder drew solace to know from his parents that they did well in the house and management of the home took care of them.

Once, the householder, because of his preoccupations, could not visit the home for long. When he visited it after a couple of months, he was surprised. He found his parents sick and emaciated. He was annoyed. He picked up argument with manager of the home on the plea that the home did not provide good food to his parents. The manager waited until the householder vented out his emotions and said:

"Your parents have become sick not because we are not providing good food to them."

"What else could be reason for their sickness?" said the householder.

"They are starving of love from you, which we cannot provide," said the manager.

The householder felt very sorry for his thoughtless action to admit his parents in the home. Immediately he shifted his parents to his own home and made them homely.

- - -

85. STREET MONGREL

A young street mongrel met with an accident. She was bruised badly. She limped, whimpered, moved to a street side and sagged sideways on ground. A householder, who witnessed the scene, took pity on the mongrel, gave her first aid, bandaged her bruised leg, took her into front yard of his house and put a bowl of milk before her. The mongrel drank the milk after some time and took rest.

Under care of the householder and his family members, the mongrel recovered very fast and became normal within a few days. She became a pet in the house and moved freely inside the house. She grew older and became a part of the house.

One day, two street dogs fought ferociously with each other in the street. The mongrel barked from inside of the house, ran into the street and tried to intervene in the fight. One of the enraged street dogs attacked the mongrel and injured her. With tooth bites all over her body, the mongrel escaped back home. Inmates of the house felt very sorry for plight of the mongrel, called a veterinary doctor home and gave treatment to the mongrel. But the mongrel did not recover from her injuries. Her condition deteriorated, day by day.

One night, when it rained, condition of the mongrel turned worse. The householder helped the mongrel take milk. But the mongrel did not touch it. She lay still in hall of the house, on a bed sheet spread by the householder. Mother of the householder saw critical condition of the mongrel and advised his son to move the mongrel out of the house, because she could die any moment and it was not auspicious for the dog to die inside the house. But the house holder did not heed advice of his mother. Late in night, he left the mongrel in hall to sleep for the night and went to bed, inside his bedroom. But, very soon, he heard strange sounds made by the mongrel. He got up, came out of his bedroom and saw. The mongrel got up, went to entrance door of the house and started scratching the door with her legs. The householder understood that the mongrel wanted to go out. He opened entrance door and let the mongrel move out. The mongrel went out of the house, moved away to a corner in the front yard, saw the householder for the last, closed eyes and sagged down lifeless.

The householder understood that the mongrel did not want to die inside the house, because mother of the householder said that it was inauspicious for the mongrel to die inside the house.

- - -

86.   THE CORRUPT TURNED HONEST

Long ago, there lived a public servant in the service of a king. He was highly corrupt. All of a sudden, he turned very honest. The man, who demanded bribes from public that approached him for his services, stopped taking bribes, altogether, and, in addition, dissuaded public from giving bribes. The public, who got used to giving him bribes, got surprised with a sudden change that came over him. Initially they suspected that either some enquiry was against him or he feared someone in the royal establishment. When nothing of that sort was found to be true, the public started praising him.

The king got a tip about the corrupt turned honest public servant in his service. He sent for the man and said to him:

"I understand that you were very corrupt earlier."

"Yes sir," said the public servant.

"Is it a fact that you have turned very honest these days?" said the king.

"Yes sir," said the public servant.

"How did such a big change come over you? Has anybody advised you or cautioned you against corruption?" said the king.

"Nothing of that sort happened," said the public servant.

"Have you changed, on your own?" said the king.

"Yes sir," said the public servant.

"But why?" said the king.

"Corruption has become too costly for me to continue," said the public servant.

"What do you mean?" said the king.

"What I get out of corruption is less and what goes out of it to others is more," said the public servant.

"Tell me more clearly," said the king.

"I am exploiting public for bribes and my superiors are exploiting me for their shares. When others are exploiting me more than I am exploiting public, I have turned honest," said the public servant.

The king laughed, told the public servant not to resort to corruption again and initiated action to root out corruption from public service.

- - -

87.   RECOGNITION

A man had deep desire for recognition. He did many works in quest of recognition. He wrote books. He acted in dramas. He sang songs. He organised religious and cultural functions. He took part in social service activities. He got into news many a time. In spite of it, he could not bag recognition that he yearned for. He was tired of running after recognition. He took it for granted that he would not get recognition in his life time. He withdrew suddenly from all public appearances and remained confined to home, doing what he was interested in, the most.

Many years passed. The man became old. He was at fag end of his life, counting his last days. One day, when he was all alone at home, someone tapped door of his house. The old man went to the door and opened it. A stranger stepped inside forcibly and said:

"How are you, sir?"

"I am sorry. I am not able to recognise you. Who are you?" said the man.

"Don't you recognise me? I am your most sought after guest," said the entrant.

"Sorry, I am not able to place you," said the man.

"You have craved to see me all throughout your life and when I come to see you at last, you say that you are not recognising me," said the entrant.

"Please excuse me and reveal yourself," said the man.

"I am recognition," said the entrant.

Meantime, the man heard on radio that he got a coveted national award in recognition of contributions made by him in various walks of life. He heard the news unemotionally. He was neither happy nor unhappy. He looked at the recognition standing before him and said to him:

"You did not come to see me, when I sought after you the most. You came to me when I stopped searching for you."

"I am like a free bird in air. If someone is trying to catch me, I fly away from reach of him. When he is not looking for me, I come, on my own, and perch on his shoulder," said the recognition.

- - -

88. FRESH LEASE OF LIFE

A man was on his death bed. When he looked back at his life, he realized that he did not do what he wanted to do at starting of his life and did many things other than that. He felt sorry to note that he was leaving the world without doing what he wanted to do. He grew remorseful. He wished how good it would be if he lived for some more time such that he could finish what he missed to do. He prayed to god. The god appeared before him and said:

"Why did you call me?"

"I am feeling very repentant to say that I missed to do what I wanted to do at starting of my life," said the man.

"What do you want from me?" said the god.

"I want a fresh lease of life," said the man.

"How long do you want to live more?" said the god.

"As long as I have lived on earth so far," said the man.

"Live on for one more life span and finish what you have missed to do," said the god.

The man was very happy. He got up from his death bed and lived on. He felt exhilarated to note that he got one more lease of fresh life. He swung back into action. He started doing many works other than what he wanted to do and what for he got fresh lease of life. He continued the same, until his second lease of life drew to an end. During entire span of second life, he did not even remember why he got second lease granted by the god. At last, when he was on his death bed again, he remembered that he missed to do what he wanted to do, a second time. At end of the life, the god appeared before him and asked if he finished what wanted to do. The man put up a blank face. The god took back the life that he gave to the man and disappeared.

- - -

89. POOR MAN'S HOTEL

A war broke out near a place, where a trader migrated to and settled. The trader could not risk staying in the place any more. He wanted to dispose off his material property and leave the place. But he found none to take his property. He left everything in the place, took his wife and son and returned to his native place, a small coastal town. He was ruined financially. He lost everything that he acquired in his place of migration. But he was not disheartened. He bought a small piece of land near cross road junction in outskirts of the town, erected a make shift shed and opened a coffee hotel there. He charged very less. He served quantities of food more than other hotels served. Daily labourers, the poor and unprivileged patronised the food centre. The food centre became a poor man's hotel.

Many rich people in the town wondered at turnover made by the hotel. They persuaded the trader to sell the hotel for whatever price he quoted. But the trader was not tempted. More than income that he got out of his hotel, he got the satisfaction that he served many people that were needy and poor. He continued to run the hotel until he turned old and died. Soon after him, his wife too passed away.

Son of the trader was a man of different mindset. he found no sense in running a hotel that paid back less and it was more profitable, if he sold the hotel for a good price and lived on interest earned out of it. He sold the hotel for a good compensation. The owner, who bought the hotel, pulled down the makeshift shed, razed everything in it to ground and erected a big hotel in the place with all modern amenities. In place of the poor man's hotel, a rich man's hotel came up. Son of the trader, who did not like to stay idle, joined the rich man's hotel as an employee. He turned from employer to employee.

- - -

90.   STRANGE BIRD ON TREE

A bird came from a distant place and perched to rest on branch of a big banyan tree in a village. Many birds that dwelt in nests on various branches of the tree came hurriedly to greet him and find out details about him. They lined up one after another. The first bird walked slowly to the new bird, introduced himself and said politely:

"I am delighted to meet you. May I know who are you and wherefrom you have come?"

"Thank you for your receptive words. I am a blue bird. I came here from a very long distance,"

"That is very nice to hear about. What caste you belong to?"

"What is caste?"

The greeter looked at the blue bird with a frown and walked away. The second bird in line came forward and repeated the same questions to the blue bird. The blue bird gave replies that he gave earlier. The second bird too walked away with scowl on his face. Thereafter, the third, fourth and other birds in the line asked the same questions and the blue bird gave the same replies. After hearing replies from the blue bird, bird after bird that dwelt on the tree walked away angrily and scornfully. The poor blue bird did not understand what went on with him.

After the episode of greeting was over, all native birds on the tree assembled in a place, discussed what to do with the casteless bird and passed a resolution. They named a brown bird to convey their resolution to the blue bird. The brown bird went to the blue bird that was in a sleepy mood and said:

"Fly away from this place this instant."

"What is the problem?" said the blue bird.

"You have no place to stay here," said the brown bird.

"Why?" said the blue bird.

"You don't have any caste," said the brown bird.

"Who said it?" said the blue bird.

"It is decision of a general body of birds staying here," said the brown bird.

The blue bird looked at the birds on tree that assembled in a place nearby, pitied them, looked at the courier, smiled, flapped his wings, rose into air and flew away.

- - -

91.   ODYSSEY OF LIFE

A group of students finished their studies in a forest school run by a saint. On the occasion of completion of their studies, the saint wanted to give his parting speech. All students assembled under a tree. The saint said to them:

"This is a momentous occasion. You have successfully finished your study phase of life here. Until you came here, your parents took care of you. During your stay here, we have taken care of you. Once you will move out of this school into world at large, there will be none to hold your hand and conduct you through life. You have to take care of yourselves, at every stage of life. The world is very large and expansive. It is the place where you can make your success. It is the place where you can encounter failure. It is a place of many chances and choices. It is there for you, if you want to make use of it. It is not there for you, if you don't want to make use of it. It is up to you whether you lead a responsible life and script your success or lose your ground and sink into abysmal depths. Be always conscious of mission of your life. Never lose sight of it. This is the last interaction between me and you. After this, you will move away from this place and go to different lands to realize your dreams. We may meet again in our life or may not. I wish you all success in your future course of life. In case you have any doubts, you may ask me."

Some students asked doubts that they had and the saint clarified them. One student asked him:

"Sir, I have a doubt."

"Tell me," said the saint.

"The world is full of rivals that come in my way, enemies that try for my downfall, obstacles that stop me from moving ahead, attractions that distract me and possibilities that fail me. With none beside me to support, can I make my journey in the world, all alone," said the student.

"Why do you think that there is none beside you in your epic journey through life?" said the saint.

"I don't think there is anyone to walk with me?" said the student.

"There is a one," said the saint.

"Who is he?" said the student.

"Your goal," said the saint.

"I don't understand you," said the student.

"If you keep your life goal before you and move towards it, no force on earth can move you away from your chartered course. Goal in your mind is the best companion that protects from all distractions, digressions and rivals," said the saint.

- - -

92. FOLLOWERS OF FAITH

There existed two faiths in a society. Followers of each faith held the view that their faith was great and greater than the other faith. They did not keep their views to themselves. They propagated their views vehemently and vociferously, to sharp reaction from followers of other faith. They conducted conclaves and conferences and deliberated on merits of their faith and demerits of other faith. There were occasions, when followers of the faiths, in total disagreement with each other, exchanged hot words and blows. Frequent fights to establish which faith was better led to utter chaos in the society.

Over the generations, the differences and dissensions between the rival groups increased manifold. Physical fights rather than worded debates became order of the day and they turned out to be a matter of common occurrence. One day, a serious argument between intellectuals of the rival groups snowballed into a war like situation. Followers of both the faiths assembled at one place with daggers drawn and ready to attack each other. With sticks in their hands, they were highly charged. A bloody fight between them could start any minute. Suddenly, two long robed mendicants appeared on the scene from somewhere and asked the parties why they prepared for a fight. Heads of both the fights explained the reason why they assembled on the fighting ground. The mendicants expressed their dismay and disapproval of action by the rivals and told them:

"If founders of your faiths happen to come to know why you are fighting for, they are sure to lower their heads in shame."

"How can you say so?" shouted both the rival groups.

"Because we are founders of the faiths that you are following," said the mendicants.

- - -

93.   LOCAL AND NON-LOCAL

Once, reports reached a king that non-locals in his kingdom prospered better than locals. The king enquired and established that there was truth in the report. He felt unhappy. He made up his mind to correct the situation. He decided to drive non-locals out of his kingdom and create chances for native people to prosper. Before implementation of his decision, he called for a meeting of his courtiers, communicated what he decided and asked his courtiers to give their opinion on his decision. Majority of the courtiers gave their consent instantly. But the chief minister did not agree. He said:

"Do not ask non-locals to leave the kingdom."

"Why do you say so?" said the king.

"They are work centres. They are enterprising. They work very hard. Without them, work can hardly move in the kingdom," said the chief minister.

"Do you mean that locals in the kingdom are not working?" said the king.

"I don't say so. I only say that non-locals work better than locals," said the chief minister.

"Prove your point," said the king.

"People, who have means of subsistence in their native places, do not think of leaving their native lands. People, who do not have means of subsistence in their native places, only move out of their native lands. People, who leave their home lands and go to new lands in search of livelihood, work very hard to establish themselves in their new places and come up in life. Invariably, they are engines for growth and drivers of development. They act like nuclei for local growth. Without them in their places, development comes to naught, since locals, who have lesser compulsions of life, work less hard."

The chief minister proved his point. The king was convinced. He refrained from implementation of the decision that he toyed with in his mind.

- - -

94.   RENUNCIATION

A learned saint established a devotional centre near a river inside a forest. He met devotees that came to see him and preached to them to inculcate spiritual way of life. He sent two of his disciples to go in two different directions, meet people on way and instil in them spirituality.

One day, he went to the places visited by his first disciple and spoke to people living there. He spoke to them and got a feel that his disciple did his job well. The people, who led earlier a highly materialistic life, adopted change in their lives and started leading more chaste and spiritual way of life. The saint was impressed and he proceeded to the places visited by his second disciple. Very soon, he came to know that if his first disciple did his job well, his second disciple did the job better. Virtually, his second disciple transformed lives of the people that he interacted with and made them highly religious. The saint observed that the people transformed by his second disciple left their worldly works, concentrated only god related matters and spent their times only in prayers and talks on religion. He could not decide how to acknowledge work done by his second disciple. He ended his tour and went back to his dwelling in forest. He called his second disciple and said:

"How did you bring about such a great change in the people that you spoke to?"

"I impressed on them importance of religious way of life and told them to get detached from worldly works," said the second disciple, feeling very proud of what he did.

"If you have advised your people to renounce worldly works, who in your opinion will do the worldly works," said the saint.

"Spirituality in my opinion is nothing but renouncing world and getting connected to god," said the second disciple.

"Spirituality is not renouncing world. It is living in the world with mind turned towards god. It is to make a man do his worldly works with a sense of non-attachment and living virtuously. Spirituality that makes a man run away from worldly works can never reach god, because work is one form of god," said the saint.

The second disciple understood true meaning of spirituality and set himself on preaching the same to people.

- - -

95. EYES SPEAK

A father noticed that his son came home late every night. On enquiry, he found that his son did something which he was not supposed to do and he came home after everyone in the house slept. He was pained. He wanted to talk to his son and advise him from doing wrong things. One day, he met his son, when he was alone, and told him to refrain from wrong doings. The son initially refused to accept that he committed anything wrong and accepted later on that he committed a mistake and he would not repeat it again.

Next day, the father said to his son affirmatively that he committed the mistake again. The son refused initially, but accepted finally. This continued for many days. Every time the father questioned and every time the son put up the same stance. The son took all precautions to see that he escaped attention of his father. But he could not make it happen. He wondered what power his father had to catch him having erred. One day, he said to his father:

"Whenever I commit a mistake, I take all care to see that I am not caught by you. In spite of it, you are able to catch me. Tell me the secret how you are able to catch me."

"The secret is in you," said the father.

"What is it?" said the son.

"When you commit mistake, you cannot see me straight into my eyes," said the father.

The son understood where the problem was. He blamed his eyes that failed him. He found no way how to control his eyes. He changed himself. He stopped doing wrong. He never gave chance to his eyes to fail him ever again.

- - -

96. TASTE OF SUCCESS

A student studied in a school. He was an average student. He studied well. But he never stood first in class in any subject. He was just a one among many students that studied in the class. He knew his capacity. He knew what he could do. He was not ambitious. He never aspired to fare better than how he fared in his studies.

Once, the student came across a teacher, who taught a language subject. The teacher taught the subject very well. He taught it so well that the student developed lot of interest in the language subject. The student studied the subject well and stood first in a class test conducted by the teacher. Standing first in the class was something that the student never dreamt of. It sprang surprise to not only the student but also others in the class, including the teacher, since the student never stood first in any subject hitherto in his academic journey. The teacher called the student in class by his name and heaped praises on him. Other students in the class followed suit and congratulated him.

The student stood out as a cynosure among the class of students. He was highly elated. He was overwhelmed with happiness. He could not contain himself. He felt buoyant. He felt as if he floated in air. He never tasted success earlier. He got success for the first time. The first stroke of success in his academic life enthused and enthralled him.

The student tasted and experienced how sweet success was. He decided to taste it again and again. And he tasted it not only in one subject, but also in other subjects. He settled down to taste nothing short of standing first in every subject in his academic career, thereafter.

- - -

97. WRONG DOING

A man was in the service of a king. He committed a mistake. The fear that he could be caught for the mistake, which he committed, haunted him. The man became restless. He passed through a strange state. He became jittery. He got irritated for every silly and frivolous reason and lost his balance. He behaved very oddly with his friends and family members. He lost appetite. He lost weight. He saw queer dreams. He saw in dreams authorities chasing him and hounding him for the mistake that he committed. He became sickly. He absented from duties frequently. He spent most of his time alone. He avoided moving in groups. He went through hallucinations. He looked at people suspiciously. He passed through a strange state of mind. The feeling of guilt so overweighed on him that he could no more bear the weight. The man felt that unless he confessed to someone about his mistake, he could not extricate himself from the tormenting pain that he passed through. He knew that in case he revealed what he did, he would be punished. But still he decided to confess his mistake and get relieved from pressure of it.

He sought interview with the king. The king granted it. The man confessed to the king what mistake he did and requested for a punishment to be awarded. The king heard the man narrate what he did in silence, thought for a while and told the man that he was forgiven. The man paid his respects to the king and went away with a relieved mind. The queen who was beside the king said to him:

"You have left the man without awarding any punishment. He may dare commit a mistake again."

"He will not commit a mistake again," said the king.

"Why do you say so?" said the queen.

"He has lived through what it is after committing a mistake," said the king.

- - -

98. COPYCAT

There lived two students in a class. One was very bright in studies. He always stood first in class. The other was not very bright. He always wanted to study as well as the first one. But he could not do it. He did not know how to do it. He decided to copy the first student and do everything exactly as the first student did. He observed the first student to know about what all he did.

The first student followed a strict discipline. He went in day time to school regularly and attended to classes without fail. He went to library in the evenings and read books of his choice. After nightfall, he went to a temple and sat there for long hours. During holidays and weekends, he went to fields to help his parents.

The second student started doing exactly what the first student did. But he did not pick up in studies. He remained where he was, even after trying to copy life style of the first student. When his attempt to pick up in studies failed, he decided to talk to the first student and get a clue on how to do well in studies. He met the first student and said to him:

"I would like to confess something to you."

"What is it?" said the first student.

"I have been trying to copy you for some time," said the second student.

"What for?" said the first student.

"In order to study as good as you are studying," said the second student.

"What are you copying from me?" said the first student.

"I am copying everything that you are doing," said the second student.

"Tell me in detail what are you copying," said the first student.

"I am attending to school regularly, going to library and temple every evening and going to fields in weekends, exactly the same as you are doing," said the second student.

"And the copying has not helped you," said the first student.

"Yes," said the second student.

"Do you know why it has not helped you?" said the first student.

"No," said the second student.

"It has not helped you because you have not copied me fully," said the first student.

"What is it that I have not copied from you?" said the second student.

"Living with studies," said the first student.

"What is it?" said the second student.

"Whether I am in school, library, temple or field, I remain connected to my studies," said the first student.

"How can you do it, when you are in temple or field?" said the second student.

"When I am in temple, I sit calmly in a corner and revise lessons that I have learnt. When I am in field, I do small physical jobs to help my parents, but my mind lives in the company of studies," said the first student.

The second student understood that he copied the first student only partially, got a clue from the first student on how to study and started living with studies as suggested by the first student. He elevated himself in studies, very soon.

- - -

99. EVIL COMPANY

There lived in a town a learned man. He wrote books. He earned reputation as a good writer. One day, when he was alone in his house, a thief broke into his house. The writer was afraid. The thief said to the writer:

"Sir, have no fear. I have not come here for a theft. I have come here to request you for a help."

"What is it?" said the learned man.

"I lived life of a thief all my life. I have acquired lot of knowledge on how to commit thefts. There is no parallel for me in this field. Before I die, I want to leave behind all my knowledge to benefit of future generations. I am not a learned man. I can't do it. I want you to write a book on art of thieving based on my past experiences. I shall provide all necessary material that you need. I promise I shall give you a handsome sum for your service," said the thief.

The learned man got tempted. He readily agreed to request of the thief. Both decided upon a place, where they could meet every day and interact.

Thereafter, both met regularly. The thief parted with experiences that he came across and what he learnt out of them. The learned man listened carefully to what the thief narrated, understood it and transformed it into words that could find place in a book. Interaction between them continued for over a couple of years. The thief exhausted his knowledge and the learned man brought out a pioneering work on how to commit thefts.

After the work, the thief gave the learned man a good sum and said to him:

"Thank you. You have really helped me. Now I can go peacefully."

Same day, the thief left the world. The learned man grieved over death of the thief, in company of whom he spent a couple of years. He preserved the work that he brought out and read it regularly. The work appealed to him very greatly. Now and then it occurred to the learned man, if he could try out what he put in the book. For some time, he checked himself from doing it. But, in course of time, the idea took over him. The learned man started experimenting with it. He took to thieving very soon and finally turned out to be a formidable thief.

- - -

100. SWAYAM SHAKTHI

Once there lived a man, who wanted to achieve something big in life. Someone told him that it was possible only with grace of god. The man decided to pray to god, went into a forest and performed austere penance for favour from god. The god, pleased with his prayers, appeared before him at last and said:

"I am pleased with your prayers. Tell me what do you want from me?"

"Make me a king of the world," said the man.

"Become," said the god.

"How can I become, unless you make me," said the man.

"Do not make me an instrument for achieving something what you want. Try it yourself," said the god.

"How can I try, unless you give me something with which I can try," said the man.

"That I have already given you," said the god.

"What is it? I am not able to understand," said the man.

"I have given you a powerful instrument of success, with which you can achieve anything in this world," said the god.

"Will you please make it clear to me what it is," said the man.

"The greatest instrument of success that I have placed in you is self. It is alter ego of me. Know it and use it. You can achieve anything and everything with it," said the god and disappeared.

The man introspected. He succeeded to spot the self lying dormant within him. He awakened the sleepy self and bade it make him king of kings. The self woke up, yawned, shook off the inactiveness that it lay in and set out compliantly to execute its master's orders. It worked out a plan of action and started acting on accomplishment of the task assigned to it.

With the help of self, the man amassed wealth, acquired a big army and set out to conquer the whole world. He fought war after war, always emerging victorious. King after king knelt down before him in defeat. Kingdom after kingdom added up to come under the yoke of his sovereign rule. The man became a king of kings of a mighty empire.

When his quest for conquests ceased, he turned to peaceful governance of his land. In course of time, complacence set in his rule. Days passed off peacefully and without any event of significance.

One day, when everything was calm and quiet, he came under the attack of an enemy. His fort came under siege. In the fight that flared up, the enemy gained upper hand. When the fall of the fort became imminent, the king escaped through an underground tunnel in the palace that opened out into a cave on a hillside, in a far off forest.

By the time the king emerged out of the cave, the day was close to drawing to an end. The western horizon was aglow with massive diffusion of crimson hue. The big shining sphere of sun was descending fast to rest in his celestial nest.

The cosmic scene created a melancholy feeling in the king. The king understood that his life too was fast ebbing out. He felt that there was no meaning left to long to live more, when he lost everything that he gained in life. He resigned philosophically to fate and slowly ascended towards top of the hill. He wanted to jump from peak of the hill and end his life. He was drowned in a sea of sadness. When he was on his way up, a seer accosted him and said:

"Where are you going up?"

"I am going up to kill myself," said the king.

"Who are you?" said the seer.

"I am a king," said the king.

"What made you decide this?" said the seer.

"I lost a war," said the king.

"What did you lose in the war?" said the seer.

"I have lost everything, my army, wealth, kingdom, power and esteem," said the king.

"Did you inherit them from your forefathers?" said the seer.

"No. I acquired them a hard way, by dint of my own long and arduous struggle," said the king.

"That means you did not possess them initially, when you made a start in life," said the seer.

"Yes," said the king.

"What are you left with now?" said the seer.

"Nothing, save myself," said the king.

"So you have lost everything excepting yourself," said the seer.

"Yes," said the king.

"And, you have lost everything that you had acquired a hard way," said the seer.

"Yes," said the king.

"I am amazed at your ignorance," said the seer.

"Why do you say so?" said the king.

"When you say that you have lost everything excepting yourself, why do you say that you have lost everything?" said the seer.

"What shall I do with myself, when I lost everything on earth?" said the king.

"What did you do with yourself, when you had nothing with you other than the self in you?" said the seer.

"I have used it to get what all I wanted," said the king.

"The self in you that got everything for you is still intact. It is the great achiever and perennial acquirer. It is alive in you. It is calling you to put it to work for you. It is ever ready, subservient to take your command. Avail of it and gain back whatever you have lost. Like a fool, do not end your life," said the seer.

The king was defenceless. He grew silent. He shut his eyes and went into rumination. A sudden realization dawned on him. The king was relieved. He cheered up. He opened eyes to see the seer. The seer was no more there before him.

The king stepped out of his inner world and entered physical world around him. He cast his glances all around. The hillside that he did not notice earlier looked charming and enchanting. A mild hillside breeze, which blew across gently, invigorated him, with soft and soothing strokes. The king enjoyed the cool air, took in deep lungful of it and felt highly refreshed. He looked up into sky, at the red orb of the sun. A part of the orb was already down the horizon. It appeared holding out a message for him that it was drowning for the day to rise again the next day. The king deciphered the message, smiled, turned back and descended the steps with a lightened heart.

He soon succeeded in invocation of his inner self to peak of its full potency, regained whatsoever he had lost and much more than that and lived as king of kings for rest of his life. In course of time, he became a legendary figure not only in his own times, but times after him. People called him Swayam Shakthi, self, an icon of power.

- - -

CONCLUSION

Literature is a coveted collection of works by erudite thinkers that have hit upon new ideas, travellers that have bagged rich experiences in their travels, writers that have created characters from real and imaginary life to tell what they want to tell the readers, poets that have produced things of beauty and authors that have authored works on which they have authority. It is a place where there are creators, both living and bygone, to present a show of what they have seen in the world, with their own eyes. It is a place that gives opportunity to visitors to see various worlds that great men have created, based on various facets of life that they have seen.

According to John Keats, a thing of beauty is a joy forever. Literature has many things of beauty in its charming world. It is a wonder world. It enthrals visitors that enter it. It puts joys heaped on a golden platter and puts it before the visitor. It gives entertainment, enjoyment, enlightenment and charges him with electrifying bouts of energy. Going on a pleasure trip to see sightseeing spots in literary world is highly enchanting. Taking a good book in hands, holding hand of author of the book, entering the world created by him and deriving joy out of it is what can only be experienced. It cannot be expressed in words.

Physical world created by the god is only one in one. But literary world created by man created by the god is many in one. It is a confluence of many worlds created by many creators. Rendezvous with literary world is a perennial source of joy.

Many people, in busy life of modern world, are living life mechanically and monotonously. They are ever busy from dawn to dusk, preoccupied with various day to day activities and running after materialistic pursuits. They are living less in physical world and more in virtual world. They are confined to living limited life and are not stepping out of their confines to living holistic life. Meeting friends, going to libraries, reading books, visiting tourist spots, spending time in leisure with family members, taking part in social and cultural activities, showing interest to know about neighbours and what is happening in the world, living up to discharging societal obligations and leading happy and contented life have become acts of the past. Peeling off from social contacts, remaining drowned in internet and mobile related activities, not living with books, not having time for personal introspection, getting obsessed with more money, more comforts and more materialistic possessions, doing repetitive and mundane works with no end and leading solitary life away from society have become order of the day, today.

People always obsessed with endless materialistic pursuits are subjected to high tension, stress, restlessness and various physical and mental ailments. In order to get relief from the ailments, they are taking recourse to many undesirable and avoidable addictions. In the process, they are bringing upon themselves mounds of more misery. They needs must realize that there is a way out to bust the stress that they are subjected to frequently and the way out is getting solace in the lap of literature.

In the great Indian epic Maha Bharatha, there is a famous episode. The episode is about burning of Khandava Vana. Once, Agni, the god of fire, developed a serious health problem. He got advice from his doctor to burn Khandava Vana, a thick forest full of medicinal plants, to get cured of his problem. Agni tried to burn Khandava. But Indra, the king of gods, under whose protection Khandava was there, thwarted efforts of Agni to burn the forest. Agni sought help of Krishna and Arjuna, two great warriors, in his attempt to burn the forest. Krishna and Arjuna gave their help. With help of the great warriors, Agni burnt Khandava Vana successfully and got cured of his problem.

For a modern man suffering from various physical and mental ailments, literature is Khandava forest. A detour into the forest is bound to rejuvenate and relieve him from sufferings. It is set to change for better mindset of the visitor and widen his horizon of thinking.

Literature is a proven curative medicine. It has a wonderful healing touch. It acts like panacea for many problems being faced by modern man. It treats him like an angel, relieves him of stresses in him and gives him solace and succour. It is advisable for one and all to live in the company of literature and harvest happiness that abounds in it to address and redress most of his problems.

- - -

Printed in the United States
By Bookmasters